Amanda's Amish Wedding

Amelia Yoder

Contents

Prologue

Through the window she could see the chaos unfolding outside. Her father and Adam scrambled back and forth to put out more chairs as guests kept arriving.

Although there had been a guest list, like any other wedding in the small community just outside Sugar Creek, Ohio, anyone and everyone turned up to join in the celebration. And in today's case, more guests than they had expected.

A smile curved Amanda Flaud's mouth, excited to share her big day with friends, family, acquaintances, and congregation members.

In the Englisch world, most people would think that eighteen was too young to commit to someone for the rest of your life. But in the traditional ways of their community, her age was nothing to be frowned upon. Besides, Amanda reasoned, why should she wait until she was older just to know what she already knew.

Aaron Smoker was the man she was meant to spend the rest of her life with.

They might only have been courting for the last year, since her baptism, but they had secretly been sweethearts for the last two years. Aaron had stolen Amanda's heart from the day he had offered her a glass of juice at a barn raising.

Until that day Aaron had simply been another young man in the community. Someone who Amanda knew from a distance but didn't know at all.

Over the next year, they had seen each other at church, community picnics, and even the odd event held by the congregation for the youth. Amanda had fallen headfirst in love with Aaron, without any doubts if he felt the same way about her. He had confirmed her feelings on the evening of her first Sunday singing. She had barely stepped out of the barn, when Aaron had touched her elbow and asked her for the privilege of driving her home.

Since that first buggy ride, everything had simply fallen into place. Their dreams for the future were perfectly aligned. They had so much in common that everything simply made sense. That was why when he had asked for her hand in marriage a few months ago, once again, Amanda didn't hesitate.

Even now, when she closed her eyes, she could see her future with Aaron. She could see them as newlyweds, in love and eager to create a home of their own. She could see them holding their first child, and years later Aaron would teach their children how to help with the chores. She could see them growing old together, looking forward to Sunday lunches with their children and their grandchildren.

A smile curved Amanda's mouth, knowing that she was blessed to have found love at such a young age.

"Amanda, are you ready? Mamm is getting everyone to take their seats." Rowena, her sister older by two years, asked as she stepped into the room.

Amanda nodded. "Jah, I'm ready. I haven't seen the bishop yet?"

"He's here. He's having a word with Aaron as we speak." Rowena smiled as she crossed the room to Amanda. "Aaron looks just as nervous as you do."

Although Rowena was older than Amanda, she had yet to find love, but regardless of that, she was overjoyed for Amanda and Aaron.

"I'm not nervous." Amanda shrugged. "Actually, I'm excited. I know we'll be living in the dawdi haus on the Smoker property for the first few years, but I can't wait to have a home of my own and a mann to care for."

Rowena chuckled. "Clearly, you're smitten. Kumm, daed is waiting to lead you down the aisle."

Amanda's stomach tightened with anticipation. "I can't believe it's finally time. I'm getting married today!"

Rowena nodded, taking both her hands. "You are, and you make a beautiful blushing bride. Mamm was right about the pale yellow dress. It compliments you."

"Denke schweschder." Amanda smiled. "Let's go."

Amanda met her parents in the living room and patiently waited while they became emotional like parents do on such an important day. After a few tears were shed and hugs were given, her mother, sisters, and brother, left to take their seats.

"Are you ready, it's not too late to change your mind." Her father asked with a kind look.

Amanda shook her head. "There's nothing to change my mind about, daed. It's fate that I become Aaron's frau."

A few moments later, Amanda and her father made their way around the house where the guests were seated. The ceremony would take place on the porch, with their guests witnessing the event on the front lawn.

Amanda looked to the porch where the bishop and Aaron stood, and she smiled at her future husband. Aaron's smile curved his mouth before a frown creased his brow. Amanda ignored it and allowed her father to lead her down the aisle.

With every step she took, she saw something change in Aaron's gaze. Fear began to gallop in her heart, that by the time she reached him and the bishop, she needed him to smile at her, to assure her that everything was going to be all right.

Her father kissed her cheek before he handed her over to Aaron. "Take care of mein dochder."

Aaron stepped back instead of taking Amanda's hand as was the custom.

Amanda's eyes widened with concern. "Aaron?"

Instead of smiling at her and taking her hand, Aaron took another step back. He glanced at the bishop before he finally met Amanda's gaze. "I can't do this, you deserve better."

Without an explanation or another word, Aaron jogged down the porch steps, before he ran around the house and disappeared out of view.

Amanda couldn't miss the confused expressions on the guests' faces as they all looked at her with pity in their eyes.

The last thing she expected on the happiest day of her life was to be left alone at the altar.

Feeling embarrassed, humiliated, and heartbroken, Amanda fled through the front door and ran to her room. She shut the door, shutting out the guests, the pity, and the pain, before she collapsed on her bed in a torrent of tears.

Chapter 1

Haunted by the Past

Eight years later...

"It's a lovely day for a picnic, jah?" Caleb Hauptfleisch asked as he flicked open the picnic blanket before laying it out on the grass.

"It is." Amanda agreed with a smile. She kicked off her shoes and sat down on the blanket. "I swear this last winter was the longest one I've ever experienced. It felt as if the cold would never leave, and the fields would never be green again." She drew in a deep breath filling her lungs with the scent of new grass and wildflowers.

"You outshine the wildflowers when you're smiling with contentment." Caleb complimented Amanda with a charming smile.

Amanda blushed slightly and looked away. "Caleb, you're too kind." She reached into the picnic basket she had packed for the occasion and turned to Caleb. "Would you like a sandwich, a brownie, or some fruit?"

Caleb shrugged. "Nothing right now, denke."

He lay back on the blanket with his head resting on his arms as he looked up at the sky. "I can't believe we're engaged. I never thought I'd met a woman who'd steal my heart and bring an end to my life as a bachelor."

Amanda laughed. "I didn't steal anything. You asked me on that first buggy ride."

"Jah, I did. After it took me months to gather enough courage." Caleb admitted with a grin. "Are your parents pleased with our engagement?"

Amanda paused for a moment. Her parents were overjoyed that she was finally courting again, and even happier that she was engaged. But today, for the first time she found herself comparing her relationship with Caleb to the relationship she had once shared with Aaron.

Everything had felt right with Aaron. She had trusted her heart and had eagerly followed its lead only to have it broken at the altar. It had taken her months before she had mustered up the courage to smile again, and years before she even considered thinking about giving courting a second chance.

After the humiliation of her almost wedding day, Amanda hadn't trusted her heart to love again, until Caleb had come along.

Amanda had been a stall owner at the Walnut Creek Amish Flea market for the last five years. She had met Caleb when he had taken the stall next to hers only a few months after she began selling her handmade soaps, lotions, and balms.

They had been friendly acquaintances and with time they had become friends. But it had only been a year ago that Caleb had asked her on their first buggy ride. At first, her feelings for him weren't as strong as they had been for Aaron, but in time she had grown affectionate towards her stall-neighbor.

Amanda wasn't concerned that her feelings for Caleb weren't as overwhelming as they had once been for Aaron, simply because she believed that her feelings for Caleb were more steady, more real.

"Amanda?" Caleb asked with a frown when she hadn't answered his question.

"Ach, sorry. I'm enjoying the fresh air so much, it's distracting. "Jah, my parents are very pleased by the engagement. I think they're eager to marry off their last dochder." Amanda teased.

"I'm sure that's not true but I'm glad they're pleased. I can't wait to become part of your family and to call you, my frau." Caleb reached for her hand and pressed a kiss to the back of it.

Amanda searched Caleb's gaze and saw nothing but devotion, affection and love there. Although she hadn't known about Aaron's doubts before their wedding, she knew in her heart that Caleb didn't harbor any doubts at all. He was eager to be married and start a family. Every time they spoke of their future Amanda was assured of his commitment to both her and their relationship.

"Me too!" Amanda said with a smile. She looked away to the trees in the distance, wondering why Aaron was on her mind that day. Usually, she managed to push him into the distant depths of her mind, but today he seemed to shove his way into the present.

It was surprising since she hadn't even laid eyes on Aaron since their unfortunate wedding day. The next day he left for Lancaster County, and Amanda hadn't heard from him since.

Perhaps that was why he was on her mind today, she reasoned. Perhaps it was because she was ready to take a step towards her future without having an explanation for what happened in the past.

"One day, we're going to come on a picnic with our kinner and we'll tell them all about how we met at the flea market and how we fell in love. I'll teach our kinner everything there is to know about pet supplies and accessories, and you'll teach them all the secrets of brewing homemade soaps." Caleb said, turning onto his side, and resting his head on a propped-up elbow.

Amanda laughed. "I don't brew soaps. You make it sound like witchery."

Caleb shrugged with a smile. "Well, judging by the scent and how well your products sell, I'm sure there's a little magic involved."

Amanda's laughter filled the air and her heart soared. This was why she loved Caleb. There might not be the thrill of excitement or sparks of attraction, but there was steady admiration that made her feel appreciated and loved.

And more than anything, she was sure of his feelings for her.

Because the last thing Amanda wanted the next time she walked down the aisle, was to be left standing there alone because her fiancée wasn't ready to commit.

With Caleb, she had no doubts and that feeling of security meant more to her than any thrills or sparks ever could.

She pushed Aaron back into the past where he belonged and focused on enjoying a wonderful afternoon with her fiancée.

Chapter 2

The Prodigal Son Returns

A aron Smoker stepped off the bus and wondered if returning to Sugar Creek had been the right thing to do.

When he had boarded a bus more than eight years ago, he had been certain that he would never step foot in this town or his childhood community again. He had spent the last eight years in Lancaster County and hadn't regretted his decision to leave for a single day in his life.

For the first two years, he had worked as a carpenter's apprentice under his uncle's guidance, and for the last six years, he had honed his skills and made a name for himself in his uncle's community. He didn't plan on coming back, he hadn't even considered it, until he received a letter from his sister, Sadie, two days before.

His father, Abram Smoker, had passed away peacefully in his sleep. The news had come as a shock to Aaron. At first, he had thought it would be best to send his condolences to his mother and sisters through a letter, but finally, he had decided to return to Sugar Creek for the funeral.

He knew there would be questions, frowns, and of course, the ghosts of the past in Sugar Creek, that would haunt him, but he needed to be there for his family.

A heavy sigh escaped him as he climbed into an Englisch cab and gave the address of his childhood home in the Amish community. Doubts overwhelmed him, but more than that fear clawed at his neck.

Being back in Sugar Creek would mean having to face Amanda Flaud.

His heart skipped a beat as guilt washed over him. He would never forgive himself for what he had done to Amanda, but he had believed it to be the right decision at the time. Even now, he still believed it had been for the best.

Perhaps if he had explained his reasons to her, or apologized before he had left, he wouldn't have carried so much guilt with him over the years. The disappointed expression in her eyes, standing on her parents' porch in her wedding dress, still haunted his dreams.

He pushed the memories of Amanda aside and tried to focus on the reason for his return.

His father's funeral.

The car stopped in front of the barn and Aaron climbed out. He looked around the homestead expecting it to have changed over the years he had been gone, but it looked the same. If he was honest, it looked a little worse for wear. The house needed a fresh coat of paint and the kitchen garden had yet to be brought back to life after the winter.

Had his father been ill?

While he was gone, he kept in touch with letters, but he now wondered how honest the letters he had received were.

The front door opened, and his sisters, Sadie and Charlotte rushed out to greet him.

Aaron set down his luggage and opened his arms to welcome them into a warm embrace.

"You came!" Sadie said standing back and searching his gaze. "We weren't sure that you would."

"It's so gut to have you back bruder. You are staying, jah?" Charlotte asked with hope in her eyes.

Aaron didn't answer their questions, but instead made his way to his mother who stood on the porch, holding onto her chest as if her heart was about to escape.

"Mamm." Aaron said stopping in front of her.

"Aaron...how gut it is to see you, seeh." Louisa Smoker couldn't stop the tears of joy if she tried.

Aaron wrapped his mother in a warm hug and held on to make up for lost time. He allowed her to weep against his shoulder, wondering how many times she had wept in his absence. "It's okay mamm, I'm here now."

When he finally stood back, he was surrounded by what was left of his family for the first time in eight years. Lancaster County had never felt truly like home, he realized now.

"Kumm, let's go make some kaffe. We have a funeral to plan." His mother finally said sniffing back her tears.

Aaron followed them into the kitchen, grateful that it still looked and smelled the same. The scent of lemon furniture oil hung in the air along with the rich aroma of freshly brewed coffee.

If anyone had to look at them now, planning their father's funeral, they looked like a perfectly normal Amish family, Aaron thought as he glanced around the table. But what no one knew was that they had a family secret, one that wasn't even spoken of in their close inner circle, a secret so big that it had torn their family apart and had been the reason Aaron had walked away from Amanda eight years ago.

That secret wasn't spoken of now.

An hour later, Sadie, who had clearly taken the lead with the funeral arrangements in Aaron's absence, sat back and put down her pen. "I think that's everything. Aaron, will you go with mamm to arrange the flowers for the coffin?"

"Jah, of course." Aaron agreed, reaching for his mother's hand.

"Sadie and I will take care of daed's things. There is a lot we can donate to the community chest." Charlotte said, turning to Sadie.

"Denke. I can't imagine taking care of that." Louisa admitted with a sigh.

Aaron's shoulders weighed heavy with the weight of his family's sorrow. He stood up and let out a sigh. "I'm going to take a walk to clear my head, if you don't mind. It's been a long day."

"Of course." His mother quickly encouraged him. "Take your time Aaron, we're just grateful to have you home."

But that was the thing, Aaron thought as he walked out of the kitchen, he wasn't sure if he was home for good yet. The family secret that had driven him away from Sugar Creek no longer mattered, but that still didn't mean Aaron was ready to move on.

His memories of Amanda flooded him and for the first time in eight years Aaron wished he hadn't walked away from his wedding day. Amanda could be married now, with children of her own, he realized with a heavy sigh of regret.

But if she wasn't, could there be a possibility of a second chance?

Chapter 3

Ashes to Ashes, Dust to Dust

Amanda stood with her family in the community cemetery. The grave was surrounded by immediate family, followed by extended family members. Next, stood the close friends of the Smoker family, followed by the rest of the community.

As she stood there, with her gaze on the ground, she realized that if things had been different, she would've been standing with the immediate family today. Due to her short stature, she couldn't see the deacon presiding over the service or the Smoker family. So instead, she kept her gaze on the ground as she listened to the brief sermon of farewell for Abram Smoker.

Ever since Aaron had left Sugar Creek Amanda had distanced herself from his family. She had always been fond of Sadie and Charlotte, but it had hurt too much to see them after Aaron had left. Now she wished they were still close because she wanted to console them in their grief. She couldn't imagine how difficult it must be to lose a parent, especially so suddenly.

"Abram Smoker was a pillar of this community. Like an ancient oak tree, he stood steadfast in his faith and weathered the storms of life. He was a dutiful father, a caring husband, and a gut friend to anyone that gave him the time." The deacon's voice carried to Amanda.

A smile curved her mouth, as she remembered Aaron's father.

"We say farewell to him today in the words of Genesis 3:19 *For dust you are and to dust you will return.* We were blessed to have known Abram and even more blessed to carry his memory with us during this time of mourning. I ask you to keep the Smoker family in your prayers. Respects can be paid at their homestead, where refreshments have been prepared for the community."

The deacon ended the service with a prayer and Amanda found herself thinking of Aaron.

As the mourners began to move away, Amanda's mind played tricks on her. Because there, right next to the grave she could swear she'd seen Aaron.

She shook her head and quickly turned to follow her parents to their buggy. Everyone was quiet on the ride to the Smoker homestead. The Smoker family didn't live far from her home and Amanda had often walked over to visit Aaron when they were younger.

But today she wasn't a guest, she reminded herself. She was nothing to this family that had almost become her own.

"It's terrible for the familye to have lost Abram so suddenly, but passing in your sleep is a peaceful way to be called home." Eli, Amanda's father said as they stopped on the Smoker homestead.

"Jah. It's just sad that they didn't have a chance to say goodbye. No warning, no idea that he would never wake up again." Sarah, her mother sympathized.

Rowena, who was now married with a family of her own, had come to the funeral with her husband. Angela, now married, had also come with her own family. It was just Rose, Amanda, and Adam, who were traveling with their parents.

"Kumm, let's go pay our respects," Eli said turning to his grown children before he climbed out of the buggy.

Amanda followed her family around the house to the porch. The deacon who held the service stood with Aaron's mother on the porch holding a cup of tea.

"Ah, there is Rowena, let's go see her first." Amanda's mother said over her shoulder before she climbed the stairs.

Amanda fell back, allowing Rose and Adam in front of her before she followed them up the porch.

"Rowena, I'm so sorry for your loss. We'll keep your familye in our prayers during this time of mourning." Louisa said, reaching for Rowena's hands.

The deacon turned and nodded in greeting to the Flaud family. Beside him stood a man, with his back turned towards them, as Amanda approached Rowena. "Mrs. Smoker, I was so sorry to hear about Mr. Smoker. My sincerest condolences for your loss."

"Denke, Amanda." Rowena smiled warmly at Amanda.

At that moment the other man turned around and Amanda felt like a rug had been pulled out from underneath her. Standing just two feet away from her was the man she had last seen eight years ago.

When he had turned and ran away from their wedding, leaving her at the altar.

Her head began to spin, certain that she was hallucinating. Her knees quivered beneath her weight, even as she caught her breath. She blinked, trying to stop her mind from playing tricks on her.

She didn't realize that a deathly silence had fallen over the porch as everyone witnessed Amanda and Aaron coming face to face for the first time since their wedding day.

"Amanda?" Aaron's voice sounded deeper.

She took a step back, completely caught off guard. Emotions washed over her like a tidal wave at his unexpected presence. He looked the same, and yet he looked different.

Fine lines were fanning out from his eyes, but his eyes still had the power to render her speechless.

Not knowing what else to do, Amanda did what he had done eight years before.

She ran.

As fast as her legs could carry her, she ran from the porch, through the gate, towards the fields that would take her home. As she ran, her entire relationship with Aaron played over in her mind, right up to the day he had walked away from her.

Her lungs burned with exertion, but she couldn't stop running.

She had imagined seeing him again for years, and she had thought of all the things she had wanted to say to him, but just now, she couldn't think of a single word.

He was back, those were the only words that kept repeating themselves in her head.

Chapter 4

Running Towards the Past

Aaron stood beside his mother and Amanda's family, but to him, the entire world had disappeared. He knew that going back to Sugar Creek would mean seeing Amanda again. He just wasn't prepared for the flood of emotions he would experience when he did.

The moment their gazes had met it had felt like no time had passed at all. His heart had swelled with love as regrets washed over him. For the first time he realized he had made a mistake and that he had wasted eight years of his life, waiting to realize it.

He wasn't about to waste another minute.

Aaron didn't even bother to excuse himself from his father's funeral before he pushed through the mourners on the porch and ran after Amanda. He knew that everyone was watching him and that the gossipmongers would have a field day witnessing him running after Amanda, but he didn't care.

All he cared about was Amanda.

He instantly recognized her voice the moment he heard her speak. He had turned around to make sure it was truly her standing beside him. He didn't expect to still love her, but the fact that he hadn't courted in eight years should've been a good indication, he thought now as he rushed through the fields after her.

How many times had he crossed this field, excited to see her and to tell her how much he cared. He was taken back to the day before their wedding when he had crossed this exact field to tell her that he couldn't wait to start a future with her.

And now…

Now he was running after her to say he was wrong. He knew no number of apologies or perfectly orchestrated words could take away the pain he had caused eight years ago, but Aaron had never been more certain of anything in his entire life.

Amanda Flaud was his future, and he was done allowing the ghosts of his past and his family's secret to drive them apart. They were meant to be together.

As he ran through the gates of their homestead, he didn't even have to guess where she would be. There was only one place she would go when she was upset, Aaron thought as he ran around the barn, towards the weeping willow behind it.

He slowed his pace when he saw her sitting under the willow on an old tree stump, they had dragged there together during their courtship. This had been her place and when they had fallen in love, it had been theirs.

"I knew you'd come to the willow…" Aaron trailed off as he approached her.

Amanda shook her head. "Go away Aaron, I have nothing to say to you." She turned her head away from him, refusing to meet his gaze.

"I have a lot I need to say to you. I owe you an apology…" Aaron began as he kneeled in front of her and reached for her hands. They were warm and soft, but he barely touched them before she jumped up and moved away from him.

"I don't care what you have to say. It's in the past, it doesn't matter now." Amanda squared her shoulders, stubborn, just like Aaron remembered her.

It broke his heart to know that he'd hurt her, but he would do everything in his power to win her back, he vowed as she stood with her back turned to him.

"Amanda please, we need to talk." Aaron pleaded.

"If I'd known you were going to be there, I wouldn't have gone." Amanda shot back with anger in her voice.

"I arrived yesterday." Aaron explained. "I'm sorry I caught you off guard. I should've known better. I should've come to see you when I arrived."

"You don't owe me anything, Aaron. And I don't owe you the time to listen to your excuses. What you did was heartless and cruel. Nothing you say can ever make me forgive you. I don't ever want to see you again. If you want to do something, do that. Make sure I never have to see your face ever again." Amanda's voice broke as she doled out her demands.

Aaron took a step back, hurt by her words.

He hadn't realized how angry she still was and knowing now that he still loved her like the day he had asked for her hand in marriage, made it hurt even more.

But it couldn't hurt as much as what he had done to her. He wanted to say the right words, to make her understand why he had walked away from their wedding, but he knew she wasn't ready to listen.

And was he ready to tell her the truth?

Half-baked excuses and made-up explanations weren't going to win her back, Aaron realized.

She wept quietly, with her back still turned to him, but Aaron knew it was too soon to touch her, or to try and console her.

Instead, he took a step back and knew she wasn't ready to listen, and he wasn't ready to tell her a secret that no one else knew.

"I'm sorry..." he said quietly, just loud enough for her to hear, before he walked away from *their* place.

As he crossed the field back to his own home, he decided that he wasn't going back to Lancaster County. This was where he belonged, and Amanda was his future.

He just needed to find a way to make her listen and make her see that they could still have everything they had once dreamed of.

But before that could happen, he needed to find a way to earn her forgiveness.

While everyone was mourning the death of his father, Aaron mourned the day he broken Amanda's heart.

Chapter 5

The Ultimate Amish Flea Market

Amanda climbed off the bus along with all the other vendors from her community and turned her face up to the warm morning sun. It simply made more sense to travel by bus to the Walnut Creek Flea Market, instead of coming by horse and buggy. Not only would it mean that the horse would need to be stabled during the flea market hours, but Amanda preferred not to drive on busy Englisch roads.

Usually, she looked forward to Thursday mornings. It wasn't as busy as the rest of the market days and gave her time to do inventory in her stall and to catch up with all the other vendors. The flea market was only open on Thursdays, Fridays, and Saturdays, giving its vendors a platform to sell their items as well as enough time at home to be with their families and make new products.

As she made her way to the blue building, she couldn't help but remember the events of the weekend.

She still couldn't believe that Aaron was back.

Her heart raced as she remembered how he had run from his own father's funeral after her. Should she have given him a chance to explain what had happened eight years ago?

She shook her head in answer to the question in her mind. Too much time had passed for her to dwell on the past. Her future was now with Caleb and that was what she should focus on.

As she approached her stall aptly named, Amanda's Amish Alternatives, a frown creased her brow noticing the stall beside her was empty. An elderly lady from a different community had been her stall neighbor for the last three years. She had sold dried herbs and spice mixtures which had been popular amongst market customers.

"Guten mayrie, mein liebe." Caleb walked out of his stall and greeted her with a bright smile. Caleb didn't sell anything handmade or authentically Amish, instead, he was a vendor for pet supplies. He bought wholesale and resold anything a pet owner could need. His stall was meticulously organized with everything from leashes, puppy-wear, treats, and toys.

"Guten mayrie, Caleb." Amanda greeted him a little distractedly. "Do you know why Wanda's stall is empty?"

"Jah, I learned from one of her friends this morning that her husband suffered a stroke. They are both moving to Lancaster County to live with their kinner. It all happened very fast." Caleb explained. "How was the funeral?"

Amanda turned to Caleb with a wide-eyed look of surprise. "What do you mean?"

Fear clawed up her spine, wondering if Caleb had heard about Aaron's return and how seeing him again had caused her to run from the funeral.

"You're a little edgy this morning, aren't you?" Caleb teased. "I just meant was it very sad, was the service heartfelt?"

Amanda quickly nodded realizing that Caleb wouldn't know about Aaron's return. She nodded with half a smile. "Jah, the service was very nice, and it was sad, as funerals are."

She couldn't help but feel a little guilty that she left out the Aaron-part of the funeral. But Aaron was in her past, she reminded herself, Caleb was her future.

"At least it's over now." Caleb assured her with a smile. "Would you like some kaffe?"

Ever since they had begun courting, Caleb brought two thermoses of coffee to the market every day, making sure he had enough for Amanda as well. "Denke, that would be nice."

Amanda walked into her stall and glanced over the shelves and displays without seeing anything. She couldn't seem to get Aaron off her mind. And although she had no interest in allowing him to explain himself, she couldn't help but wonder what excuse he thought would make her forgive him after all this time.

She picked up a dusting wand and began to dust the shelves, making sure her products were dust free. Her mind was too distracted to focus on doing a stock count, but at least she could be productive, she assured herself.

Amanda's Amish Alternatives was one of the few stalls at the flea market that sold completely unique products. There was no other stall like it, and on busy days she was overwhelmed by the amount of interest.

It had all begun when Rowena had a rash as a teenager. Amanda's mother had tried lotion after lotion to soothe the eczema that had irritated Rowena's skin until Amanda stumbled across a recipe in her grandmother's medicine book.

For years their family had turned to the medicine book for remedies like snake juice for the flu and poultices, but no one had ever paged through to discover the balms, lotions and soap recipes that had been hidden between the pages.

The balm she had made for Rowena's eczema had worked like a charm and to this very day, Rowena still used it. So, when the time came for Amanda to think of a way to earn an income, she began to sell homemade balms, ointments, and soaps in the community. It had been her mother who had encouraged her to take a stall at the flea market, and Amanda hadn't looked back since.

The eczema balm she named *Lavender Bee* was her bestseller to this day. The range had begun with the balm and had now expanded with soaps, lotions and even shampoo for eczema prone skin. It was a simple recipe of shea butter, almond oil, tea tree and lavender oil, along with a few other calming natural ingredients, but it worked like no other remedy available.

Over time, Amanda played with different fragrances and developed different ranges from her customers' requests. She had started making scented candles as well. As one of her Englisch customers had once said, stepping into Amanda's stall was like stepping into fragrance heaven.

But this morning her mind wasn't on her products or how well they worked, her mind was firmly distracted by a man she thought she would never see again.

"Here you go, mein liebe." Caleb suddenly said beside her.

He startled Amanda, interrupting her thoughts, making her jump almost a mile high. "Ach Caleb, you gave me a fright."

"Is everything all right, you seem a little off this morning?" Caleb asked concerned.

Amanda knew he was trying to be kind, but the only thing she needed from him this morning was a little space. "Nee, I'm fine." Amanda insisted.

"Are you sure? If I did something to upset, you..." Caleb trailed off with a questioning look.

Amanda shook her head. "I said I'm fine, I just need to focus on my stall today, all right?"

With that, Caleb shrugged with a curious look before he returned to his own stall. Luckily the market opened only ten minutes later and unlike a usual Monday morning, it was busy enough to excuse Amanda from making small talk with Caleb for the rest of the day.

Chapter 6

Time for Permanence

It had been two weeks since Aaron and his family had put his father to rest.

For the first time in his life, it felt as if he could breathe without having to hold his breath for what might happen next. Although he had spent the last eight years in Lancaster County, he still spent a lot of hours worrying about his family at home.

There had been a time when he had thought that Lancaster County was where he would build a future but being back home in Sugar Creek only confirmed what he had known all along. Lancaster County would never be his home. He had sent the rest of his things to Lancaster County the week before and just this morning a courier company had dropped off his boxes.

It had been expensive since most of the boxes contained his handcrafted wood items, but worth the cost. Besides, Aaron reasoned, he had lived frugally the last eight years and whatever endeavor he was going to start in Sugar Creek to earn an income, it would be good to have examples of his work.

It was wonderful to be home again. To be able spend time with his mother and his sisters and catch up on everything he had missed in their lives. Both his sisters had gotten married in the time he had been gone and constantly ragged on him for still being a bachelor.

Aaron didn't mind, he enjoyed every minute of being surrounded by his family again, like tonight when both his sisters and their husbands had come to join them for a family dinner. His mother had outdone herself with a roasted leg of lamb, a variety of vegetables and the fluffiest mashed potatoes that anyone could dream of.

"When are you planning on returning to Lancaster County?" Charlotte asked her brother sitting beside her. She had married a crop farmer while Aaron had been away, but luckily, she only lived a couple of homesteads away. "Samuel and I have been talking, and we thought it's best if we move in with mamm for the time being. It's not gut for her to be alone right now."

"Actually," Aaron's mother, Louisa, answered on his behalf. "Aaron isn't going back to Lancaster County. He sent for his things this week. My seeh is home for gut."

"Really?" Sadie asked with a bright smile. "You're staying?"

Aaron nodded at Sadie. Her husband of five years sat beside her, their three-year-old son on his lap. "That's gut news. That means you'll be here when we have our next boppli."

"Are you with child?" Aaron asked with delighted surprise.

"Jah, only four months along, but you'll be here when this one comes." Sadie said with delight.

"Then you'll be staying with mamm, that's gut." Charlotte said with a nod. "It's gut to have you home bruder."

Aaron nodded in agreement. "It's gut to be home."

No one spoke of the reason or circumstances he left. Their family secret was safely guarded although Aaron wished that he had the courage to tell Amanda at least. Perhaps then she would understand.

"We can have many more family dinners," Louisa said with a contented sigh. "And Aaron has begun fixing up everything around the house your daed didn't get to. He's going to paint the house next."

"Gutness, bruder, but you are busy." Sadie said with an impressed look.

"It needs to be done." Aaron shrugged. "It's what I'm going to do next that I'm worried about. In Lancaster County I had a sturdy client base that provided a regular income from my carpentry. Here, I'm afraid, no one even knows what I'm capable of."

"Then get a stall at the flea market." Charlotte suggested eagerly. "That way you can showcase your work and take on commissions. I take it you make furniture as well?"

"Jah, anything and everything as long as it's wood. I had some of my smaller items sent over from Lancaster County earlier this week. Sets of book ends, spice racks, cookbook stands, diamond shelves, ach you know, things like that." Aaron explained.

"So, you have enough things then to display in your stall already. And you could make your stall a working stall, one of those where the Englischers can watch you work." Sadie suggested. "Maybe even make a few pieces of furniture as examples so you can get commission work faster."

Aaron's brow furrowed as he thought it over. Simply being a stall vendor wasn't something he would enjoy at all. But if he had a working stall, like the one that Sadie suggested, it might just be exactly what he needed. That way he could have a workshop at home for the demanding tasks and the less demanding tasks he could do in his stall whilst demonstrating his skill and selling his other items.

"Do you think they'll allow for a working stall? Won't the sawdust and noise be a problem?" Aaron asked considering it.

Sadie's husband shrugged. "They have quite a few working stalls. I think if the noise isn't too loud and you clean up after yourself, it shouldn't be a problem. I can take you to see the organizers tomorrow if you like?"

Aaron nodded feeling hope bloom in his chest. Coming back to Sugar Creek had felt right, but now for the first time in years, it felt as if he could finally look to the future and make his plan. He only realized now that Lancaster County had always been a temporary escape from his real life.

It was now time for him to put down some roots and aim for some permanence.

Chapter 7

When Past and Present Collide

T he following Thursday, Amanda looked forward to seeing Caleb at the market. They hadn't made time for a buggy ride over the weekend and although their wedding needed to be planned, she was grateful for the time alone. It gave her the chance to work through the shock of seeing Aaron again and refocus her attention on Caleb and their future together.

She carried a box of balms and ointments in her hand which she had made during the days before to restock her stall, eager to see Caleb. She wanted to make up for being so distant the week before and had even baked him his favorite cherry pie as an apology.

As she approached her stall, she noticed that the empty stall beside her was now stocked with everything you could think of in wood. There were the most beautiful frames, spice racks, shelves and so much more, that she vowed to stop by and meet the new vendor and compliment him or her on their work later in the day. Whoever the new vendor beside her was, they weren't there at the moment.

Being earlier than usual, Caleb wasn't there yet either. Amanda restocked her shelves and did some light dusting when a voice coming from the new stall made a shiver run down her spine.

Her heart skipped a beat as she moved out of her stall to make sure her ears weren't deceiving her.

They weren't.

There, in the middle of the stall, stood Aaron, thanking one of the organizers for the privilege of becoming a vendor of a flea market. For a moment, she felt frozen, just like that day of his father's funeral on the porch.

Aaron turned around and spotted her standing there. "You're the *Amanda* from *Amanda's Amish Alternatives?*"

Aaron looked just as surprised as she was, to see her there.

"You're the new vendor?" Amanda accused him as if he had committed a crime.

At that moment Caleb walked up to her, but Amanda was too furious to even acknowledge his presence as she waited for Aaron's answer.

"Jah. Aaron's Amish Carpentry." Aaron nodded with a tentative smile. "This is a surprising coincidence, or perhaps its fate?"

Amanda felt her blood boil with anger. She had just managed to shove Aaron far back into the dark depths of her mind and into her past where he belonged. She had been certain that he would've returned to Lancaster County by now, but instead, here he was, at the Flea Market in the stall right beside hers.

"It's not fate, I stopped believing in fate a long time ago. Or did you just happen to forget?" she snapped at him, with her hands on her hips.

Aaron walked towards her and met her gaze. The sparks and attraction collided with the pain and the anger she felt with his presence. "I didn't forget anything Amanda, least of all you."

"That doesn't matter. You shouldn't be here. I was here first. You can't have this stall. You need to leave." Amanda said demandingly.

"I can't, this is all they have available. And like the organizer just assured me, they endeavor to give Amish folk the opportunity to display their talent. I see you've expanded your talent for making balms and lotions. It smells amazing." Aaron said with an easy smile.

"Amanda?" Caleb asked concerned beside her.

Amanda shook her head. "Not now, Caleb." She held Aaron's gaze. "You can't just come back as if nothing happened. You can't just pretend like the last eight years didn't happen, Aaron. It's not fair!"

Aaron sighed. "Amanda, please if you'd just let me explain."

Amanda narrowed her eyes. "I'm not wasting another minute of my time on you. Besides, I shouldn't really be worried, because you've proved that you're unable to commit." She waved towards his stall. "This won't last long. Soon enough you'll get tired of the commitment and run away like you always do."

"That's not what happened." Aaron argued.

Amanda turned her back and rushed back to the safety of her own stall. Not even the calming scent of lavender and geranium could stop her heart from racing. Anger and fear rushed through her veins, struggling to see which one was going to win. Would it be anger at Aaron for hurting and humiliating her, or would it be fear of his proximity?

"Amanda, are you all right? Who is that? What just happened?" Caleb asked gently as he moved to her side.

Amanda shook her head. "It doesn't matter, Caleb."

"Clearly it does." Caleb argued moving in front of her and searching her gaze. "I've never seen you that angry or upset before. You've met before today I presume?"

Amanda sighed. "Jah, Caleb. We've met. But it was a long time ago and it doesn't matter. I just... He doesn't belong here."

Caleb ran a hand down her arm and held her gaze. "I'm here if you need me, you hear me? And when you're ready... I'd like to hear what happened a long time ago?"

Amanda nodded, grateful that he didn't push her for more answers now. She was too upset to even comprehend what had just happened.

The last thing she expected when she had come to the flea market this morning was for her past and her present to collide without warning.

Chapter 8

Advocating for Advice

Aaron's first day at the flea market had gone better than he ever could've expected. He sold four items on his first day and even received his first commission to make a set of cutting boards for an Englisch customer.

And yet, he didn't feel triumphant at all. Instead, he felt as if he had invaded Amanda's space and ruined any chance of ever winning her heart over again.

On his way home, he knew he needed some advice. It was hard to talk to his mother about Amanda because his mother felt guilty because of Aaron's decision to run from his own wedding. It wasn't her fault, but no matter how many times Aaron had told her that, she still disagreed.

So instead of going straight home, he stopped by Sadie's homestead first. As if sensing that he needed to talk to his sister, Sadie's husband took their son with him to do the evening chores.

"What's wrong?" Sadie asked as soon as she joined Aaron at the kitchen table with a glass of homemade lemonade. "Didn't it go well at the flea market?"

Aaron shrugged with a heavy sigh. "It went better than expected." Aaron admitted. "I just didn't know the perfectly located stall I was assigned was next to Amanda's."

Sadie gasped. "Ach nee. I knew she had a stall there, but the flea market is so big I thought it would be weeks before you ran into each other."

"Try first thing this morning. She was furious, Sadie. But more than furious she looked... upset. Almost as if I had chosen that stall intentionally to taunt her." Aaron shook his head. "She even insinuated that I won't be there long because I can't commit."

"Ouch." Sadie flinched. "That must have hurt."

"It did. And what hurt more, was hearing her laugh with her customers while she ignored me for the rest of the day." Aaron admitted.

Sadie frowned. "What is bothering you more, the fact that she was angry or the fact that she didn't laugh with you?"

Aaron had never been one to talk about his feelings, except to Amanda, and even then, he hadn't been completely honest. But right now, he needed advice from someone who understood his reasons for leaving. "I don't know, Sadie. The truth is, I thought I'd come back and see her, and it wouldn't bother me in the least. It happened almost a decade ago... But the moment I saw her at daed's funeral... Sadie, it was like no time had passed at all. I still love her, I never stopped loving her. Not for a single day."

Sadie's eyes widened with surprise. "What are you saying, Aaron, do you want her back?"

Aaron didn't hesitate. "I want nothing more than to have Amanda back in my life. I want to make up for lost time and I want to prove to her that I'm not afraid of commitment... that wasn't the reason that I left."

Sadie sighed. "Ach bruder, my heart goes out to you. I can't imagine loving someone all this time and not being with them. Do you think she still has feelings for you?"

"I don't know, Sadie. But... perhaps the fact that she was so upset to see me at the funeral and again today... it gives me hope..." Aaron said hopefully.

Sadie nodded. "I agree. If she didn't have feelings for you, anger, love or otherwise, she wouldn't have been so upset by your return. The question is, are you ready to tell her the truth. Because without telling her the truth, she will never forgive you for leaving."

Only his mother and his sisters knew the true reason Aaron had run from his own wedding eight years before. Although he had managed to slay his own demons that still didn't make it easy to reveal their family secret and to tell Amanda the truth.

"I'm not sure I can do that." Aaron confided in his sister.

Sadie reached for his hand and met his gaze. "The truth can't hurt anyone anymore. You can't let your past dictate your future Aaron. You already allowed it to steal too much time from you, don't let it steal another minute. If you love Amanda and you want to win her back, you'll need to tell her that. And you'll need to tell her why you ran."

"What if she doesn't feel the same way about me?" Aaron asked, fearing the worst.

Sadie smiled at him. "Then at least you know you tried, and you can move on with your life. But I have a feeling that you've got your mind set on Amanda Flaud."

"I didn't know that was the case until I saw her again. I honestly thought she was in the past. But now, being back home, seeing her again... It's her Sadie, it's always been her." Aaron admitted out loud for the first time since returning to Sugar Creek.

Sadie's smile broadened as she squeezed his hand. "Then you just need to be brave enough to tell her the truth. I'll pray that she finds forgiveness in her heart."

"Denke schweschder. Until I do... find the courage and the time to talk to her, what do I do?"

Sadie shrugged. "Just be you. That's who she fell in love with the first time, and I guarantee you, that's who she'll fall in love with again."

As Aaron walked home from Sadie's place, he wondered what it meant to just be him. Should he ignore her anger and pretend like nothing was wrong? Or should he give her the space she needed to accept he was back, and hope that in time anger wouldn't be the only thing in her eyes when she looked at him?

Aaron wasn't sure, but he knew that until he won Amanda's heart back, he would pray every night that the Lord would guide his actions and his words.

Chapter 9

Embrace the Future

"Kumm, into bed you go," Amanda said picking up her niece before taking her nephew's hand. Babysitting her nieces and nephews was something she enjoyed more than anything in the world.

If she was honest, Amanda had thought by the age of twenty-six she would've already been a mother. But her fate had changed the day Aaron had run from their wedding. Luckily, she had her nieces and nephews to love and spoil until she was blessed with a family of her own one day.

Rowena and her husband attended the once-monthly marriage prayer meeting. In Englisch's terms, it might be considered a date night, but except for not having the children present, it was nothing like a date night. Married couples throughout the community met at the bishop's house and spent the evening talking about the challenges of marriage, raising children, and living a faithful Amish life. Rowena swore it was the only reason she still loved her husband after having two children within four years.

One day, Amanda imagined she would encourage her husband to attend the meeting as well.

She put her niece in the crib, which she was growing out of fast, and her nephew in his bed, before she picked up the book with bible stories for children. She began to read the story of Jonah and the whale, and both children were asleep before she reached the end.

She put out the lantern and made her way to the kitchen for a cup of tea. It wouldn't be long before Rowena and her husband returned, and Amanda looked forward to a little time on her own. The last couple of weeks had been more disturbing than she ever could've imagined. She had never expected Aaron to return to Sugar Creek and seeing him at the flea market for three days a week made it even worse.

Every time she saw him, she was reminded of her wedding day, before she was flooded with the memories of the courtship they had shared before that day. To this day, Amanda couldn't fathom how she hadn't seen that Aaron wasn't fully committed. She might be angry at Aaron, but she blamed herself for not realizing he wasn't in love with her in time to stop the humiliation that had been her wedding day.

She went over their last interactions, trying to find anything he said, or did that would've indicated that he wasn't ready for marriage. And the more she searched for the archives of her memories, the more frustrated she became.

Because he hadn't given her any warning at all.

"You look downright furious," Rowena commented as she walked into the kitchen. "I hope the kinner didn't give you too much trouble."

Amanda had been so lost in her own thoughts she hadn't even heard her sister and her husband return. "Nee, nee, the kinner were angels as usual. Went to sleep without any trouble at all."

"Then what's got you frowning as if you're trying to force a canyon into your forehead?" Rowena asked to help herself with some tea.

Amanda let out a heavy sigh.

"Aah, I recognize that sigh. Aaron Smoker." Rowena said taking a seat beside her sister. "Mamm said he has stall next to you at the flea market."

"Jah." Amanda rolled her eyes. "He disappears for eight years and now suddenly he's everywhere."

"Eight years is a long time." Rowena mused to herself over her cup of tea.

"Jah, it is." Amanda agreed. "And yet every time I look at him, it feels like it happened only yesterday. I don't know Rowena but having him back... it bothers me. I was perfectly fine, moving on with my life, meeting Caleb and dreaming of our future and now..."

"Do you doubt your feelings for Caleb?" Rowena asked gently.

Amanda fervently shook her head. "Nee, of course not. Caleb is nothing like Aaron. He's reliable and honest and I have no doubts about our future together."

"Then why does Aaron's return bother you?" Rowena queried.

Amanda thought for a moment and finally let out a heavy sigh. "That's the thing I don't know. I'm angry with him all over again for what he did to me. He should've been honest. And I'm angrier that he left without an explanation or an apology. And I'm even angrier that I'm allowing his return to bother me at all."

Silence hung over the kitchen for a while before Rowena finally spoke. "I wouldn't know the first thing about what you went through back then or what you're going through now, but I do know that you were crushed. It was hard to stand by and not be able to make things better for you. The only reason I can imagine that you're upset by his return, or bothered by it, like you say, is that you're not over him. Are you, over him?"

Amanda's eyes widened with horror. "Of course, I'm over him!"

"If that's the case, then seeing him shouldn't really bother you at all, should it? Besides, you have Caleb now?" Rowena asked with an innocent look.

Amanda let out a sigh, fearing her sister was right. Why did Aaron's presence bother her? She had a bright future lined up with Caleb, one that she could rely on. Aaron shouldn't be able to affect her mood or her feelings if she didn't feel anything for him, should he?

Fear trickled over her nerves, making her wonder if her sister wasn't perhaps right.

She changed the subject to the children, not wanting her sister's further analysis of her feelings for Aaron, but when she walked home, she thought of nothing else.

Eventually, she did the only thing she could, she prayed for guidance, hoping that the Lord would help her understand not only her feelings but that he would help her make peace with her past and embrace her future.

Chapter 10

Finding the Positive in a Brief Pause

Monday and Tuesday, Aaron had picked up some of the yard work around the homestead. It was clear his parents were growing older and no longer kept their hand on the chores as they used to. He didn't blame them, but the work needed to be done.

From mowing the lawn to straightening the garden beds and weeding the kitchen garden, Aaron was busier than he expected to be. By Wednesday morning there were still a lot of things he wanted to deal with before the market opened again on Thursday, but there was something else he wanted to do first.

Amanda had been on his mind since he last saw her on Saturday. The cold glances she shot his way, which encompassed more pain than anger, made him feel terrible. He had carried the guilt of hurting her for all these years but seeing her again and knowing how much he had hurt her was something he hadn't been prepared for.

Especially because he was still in love with her.

He needed an excuse to see her, away from the market. He needed a chance to talk to her, if not about the past, then at least to try and clear the air. But Aaron knew showing up at the Flaud homestead would be frowned upon, unless he had a very good reason.

So, Wednesday morning Aaron decided to make a reason. He spent the whole day using his skills and some of the best wood he had brought from Lancaster County to make her something she didn't have. Something he knew she would appreciate.

It was late afternoon when he finished carving the last word. He stood back and admired his work, knowing that the Amanda he had fallen in love with would appreciate not only his craftsmanship but the use she would have for it.

He loaded it onto his wagon and headed over the Flaud homestead, his heart racing in his chest with anticipation for what Amanda's reaction would be to his unexpected visit.

As he stopped in front of the barn, he was overwhelmed with memories of the numerous times he had visited there. There had been a time when this had been like a second home to him, but he only had to see her father stepping out on the porch with a curious look to know that eight years had changed everything.

"Aaron?" Eli Flaud asked, making his way towards him. "Of all the company that drops by unexpectedly, you're the last I expected to see."

"Hullo Mr. Flaud. I'm sorry if this isn't a convenient time." Aaron apologized outright.

"That depends, are you here to make amends or more trouble?" Eli asked with a cocked brow.

Aaron let out a sigh. "I can't change what happened in the past Mr. Flaud, but I assure you I'm not here to make trouble. I was hoping to have a word with Amanda?"

Eli searched his gaze for a moment and shook his head. "I've been angry with you for so many years and if it were my choice, I would've chased you from my property without question. But Amanda's a grown woman, she needs to decide for herself if she wants to see you or not."

Eli walked away but not without giving Aaron a warning look. Aaron couldn't blame him.

A few moments later Amanda came out of the house with a confused expression. "What are you doing here?"

"Hullo Amanda." Aaron summoned a smile. "I see not much has changed."

"Everything's changed." Amanda said through gritted teeth, stabbing him right through the heart with her words. "You're not welcome here Aaron."

"I don't intend to stay." Aaron pointed out; grateful he hadn't come empty-handed. "I noticed at the flea market; that you're running out of display space. Not surprisingly, given how busy your stall is. My mamm and schweschders swear by your products." Aaron moved around the wagon and lifted the sheet he had covered the display rack with. "I thought you could use something like this. Maybe use it for special offers, or just to display more of your products. You can move it around, as it's not heavy at all."

Aaron lifted the display rack off the wagon and set it down on its feet. There were three tiers, giving her ample space to display her goods and at the top, there was a sign with *Amanda's Amish Alternatives* carved into the wood.

Amanda's eyes narrowed before they softened. She stepped forward and let her fingers trail over the carved words as a gasp of delight escaped her. When she turned to look at him, she was the Amanda he remembered. There was no anger or pain in her eyes, just joy, like the day he had asked for her hand in marriage. "Aaron, this is beautiful. It's exactly what I need." Amanda all but gushed.

Aaron felt the praise settle over him like a warm blanket. "I thought so. I'm glad you like it."

She suddenly took a step back, and her eyes were clouded with all the years that had passed again. "Why did you do this?"

"Because I wanted to." Aaron said simply. "I know I can never make up for what I did, but I still care about you Amanda." Aaron began, hoping that Gott would give him the right words he needed to explain to her what had happened eight years ago.

Amanda shook her head and held up her hand to silence him. "Nee, you shouldn't be here. Aaron, it's not right. I'm engaged to be married. Whatever happened between us is in the past."

Aaron frowned as disappointment washed over him. "You're engaged? To whom?"

"To Caleb, at the flea market. He sells the pet supplies." Amanda let out a sigh and took another step back. "I don't want to see you again Aaron. It hurts too much. You shouldn't be here, and you should never come here again."

It felt as if he had been slapped. But instead of flinching Aaron took a step forward, wanting to fight for what he knew was right. "Does he make you happy Amanda. Tell me that you love him as you loved me, and I'll never bother you again."

Amanda's eyes widened but she paused for a moment before she answered. "It's none of your concern if I'm happy or not, but jah, I am happy. And unlike you, I don't get engaged without loving someone."

If her words had stung before, they stung even more now. He took a step back and searched her gaze, struggling to understand if he could ever win her back when there was so much hurt in her heart for him.

"You should go." Amanda said firmly.

Aaron started towards his wagon, but Amanda stopped him. "Take that with you."

Aaron did as he was told and loaded the display rack into the wagon before he drove away. He remembered the joy on her face and decided he'd take it to the flea market for her, leave it in her stall and let her decide if she wanted to use it or not.

His heart felt crushed by their interaction but the more he went over it in his head, the more he realized she had hesitated.

If she really loved Caleb how she thought she loved him and was happy, she wouldn't have hesitated, he realized with a smile.

And if he no longer mattered to her, his presence shouldn't bother her.

Filled with a glimmer of hope, Aaron returned home, knowing patience was going to be key if he wanted to win Amanda back.

Chapter 11

Comparisons Only Cause Confusion

Amanda had looked forward to her buggy ride today the whole week. Ever since Aaron had returned, she hated that he was more on her mind than her fiancée.

A few weeks ago, she wouldn't even have considered the possibility that Aaron would ever return to Sugar Creek, and now that he was here, he was stirring up the past as well as confusing emotions for Amanda.

She trusted in her heart that spending the afternoon with her fiancée would not only reassure her of her feelings for Caleb, but it would confirm that Aaron was nothing but history to her heart.

"I've been counting the minutes since I said goodbye to you at the flea market." Caleb admitted as Amanda climbed into the buggy.

They had both worked at the flea market that morning but agreed to meet at five o'clock for a late afternoon buggy ride. Her parents didn't argue, since they were happy that she had finally moved on and was once again engaged.

"Jah, me too. It's been so busy at the flea market all week; we've barely had some time for each other." Amanda agreed as she took her seat.

Caleb took the reins and called to the horse. "Step up."

Amanda glanced over the horizon as the sun began its descent. The clouds were painted in hues of grey and purple as the day began to fade. Her mind played tricks on her, and she suddenly remembered a buggy ride she had been on with Aaron when he had told her that they reminded him of the hue of her eyes. Amanda had still laughed as she explained to him her eyes were bluer than violet, but Aaron had disagreed and insisted when she looked at him with an affectionate gaze, they were more violet.

"How's the dress coming along?" Caleb asked interrupting her thoughts.

Amanda turned to him with a confused expression before she realized he meant her wedding dress. Her heart skipped a beat as guilt washed over her. Here she was thinking of another man, when she should be thinking about her wedding. "Mamm will start on it next week. We only decided on a color today."

"It would be wrong of me to guess the color, jah?" Caleb chuckled.

Amanda smiled, but it didn't reach her eyes. Choosing the right color for her wedding dress had been more troubling than she had imagined. Her previous dress had been a pale yellow and it had suited her complexion beautifully. But she refused to wear a yellow dress again. Amanda didn't believe in bad omens, but surely it wouldn't be right to wear another yellow dress considering what happened the first time around.

Her sisters had suggested blue, violet, and even a pale peach, and yet none of the colors had felt right to Amanda. It had been her mother who had finally suggested white.

Traditionally, Amish brides wore a pale purple or blue dress, but in recent years they opted for lavender, pink or green, sometimes even yellow. Wearing a white dress was almost unheard of but not against the rules of the ordnung.

The style would be plain, much like her plain dresses, but with a few buttons at the neck to make it elegant. Unlike the Englisch, Amish bridal wear didn't encompass lace or any adornments, but instead was mostly plain, like their daily wear.

Amanda hadn't agreed to the white because it signified innocence, but rather because for her it signified a clean slate. A new beginning.

Exactly, what she was looking for in her life with Caleb.

She wanted to finally put the pain of the past behind her. She wanted to forget about the humiliation and the disappointment and the lack of sympathy that followed her for months after her failed attempt at getting married.

With Caleb, she wanted a fresh start.

"My mamm has expanded the guest list for the wedding. It seems things are coming together now. I can hardly wait for the big day." Caleb said to her with an excited look.

"Me either." Amanda smiled weakly.

"Do you have any familye coming from other communities?"

"Nee. Most of our familye lives here in Sugar Creek." Amanda answered thinking about Aaron. Would he be coming to the wedding?

Although there were official invitations sent out, everyone in the community was welcome at the wedding.

Did that count for a previous beau as well?

"I thought that we could start bringing over your things to our homestead in the days before the wedding. Your trousseau chest to start with. My mamm has bought us new curtains for our bedroom and even linens for the guest room. Although it hopefully won't be a guestroom for long."

Amanda nodded eagerly although for the first time she felt a little doubtful. Should she be thinking of Aaron while she was on a buggy ride with Caleb?

"I've been wanting to ask you, but there wasn't really an opportunity at the flea market. How do you and Aaron know each other?" Caleb asked with a curious smile.

Amanda's heart skipped a beat. The last thing she wanted to discuss was her past with Aaron. "Ach, it doesn't really matter."

"Considering how furious you were with him; it matters to me." Caleb said gently.

Amanda let out a sigh. She could insist it didn't matter, but wouldn't it be better for Caleb to learn about her past with Aaron from her rather than discover it through someone else?

"We were engaged to be married." Amanda confessed. "It was more than eight years ago. He left without saying goodbye or giving me a reason and hasn't been back since."

"He just left?" Caleb asked, surprised. "That's... cruel."

"Jah, it was." Amanda admitted. "But it was long ago, and it doesn't matter anymore, but I still don't want to have to see him every time I go to the flea market."

"I can understand that." Caleb nodded in agreement. "I'm sorry he hurt you, Amanda. I can promise you I never will. I love you with all my heart." Caleb reached for her hand and squeezed it gently.

Amanda offered him a grateful smile. As she met Caleb's gaze, she couldn't help but compare the two men. Caleb was easy going and understanding whereas Aaron was stubborn at times and tended to turn to humor instead of revealing his emotions. Caleb made her feel safe and secure whereas Aaron made her feel excited and confident.

They were different in almost every aspect of their personalities, and for the first time Amanda wondered if that was why she had been driven to Caleb in the first place. Was it because he was the opposite of Aaron?

"I noticed you have a new stand for your soaps. Did your daed make it?" Caleb asked, trying to fill the silence.

Amanda shook her head. "Nee, Aaron did." She shrugged trying to make light of it. "Probably his way of apologizing for what happened back then. Not like it even matters to me, anymore." She quickly added to try and convince Caleb that it didn't.

Or was she trying to convince herself?

Chapter 12

A Community Welcome

After Sunday service the bishop had invited the whole community to a picnic on his homestead. It happened at least once every three months to get the community to socialize and stay connected with each other.

This time of year, the opportunity was mostly used to discuss who needed help with their harvests and when the men would be harvesting which farms. Farming in an Amish community often meant not having any farmhands during the year, but relying on your neighbors, friends and family when it came time to harvest.

It had been the same in Lancaster County, but unlike there, here Aaron knew everyone. As the afternoon progressed it almost felt like a welcome back celebration for his return. Anyone and everyone welcomed him home.

"Aaron, here you are. I've been waiting for a moment to talk to you alone." The bishop said as he joined Aaron. "I'm so happy that you're home. Your mamm and daed have missed you terribly. Hopefully, you've learned a lot during your time as your uncle's apprentice in Lancaster County."

Aaron nodded with a smile. The lies they told to conceal the truth about his reason for leaving had become second nature to him. "Jah, my uncle was very patient with me. Taught me everything he knew."

"Gut, gut. My frau has been hounding me about new rocking chairs for our porch. The ones we have belonged to my grosspappi." The bishop laughed. "As you can imagine, they're a little worse to wear after almost a century. I was hoping you'd be open to being commissioned to make us new ones?"

"I'd be happy to." Aaron smiled.

"Your daed would be proud of you. Just a shame he didn't have a chance to see the man you've become before Gott called him home." The bishop said with an empathetic smile.

Aaron nodded. "It would've been gut to be able to see him one last time."

He talked with the bishop a little while longer before the bishop excused himself to talk to someone else.

Aaron had barely taken a few steps when his mother's brother approached him. "Aaron, seeh. How gut it is to have you back. Your mamm must be overjoyed."

"Jah, she is, uncle. How have you been? It looks like you still have your health to be grateful for?"

His uncle chuckled as he patted his belly. "Too gut. And I also have five grandchildren that I'm grateful for. You'll meet them all yet."

After talking to his uncle for a while longer, Aaron felt thoroughly welcomed back. All his friends from before he left stopped by to welcome him. He was introduced to their wives and children and already knew he would forget all their names before the day was over.

Unlike Amanda, no one questioned him about leaving. According to the entire community Aaron had left to be a carpenter's apprentice.

No one asked about his reasons for standing Amanda up on their wedding day, or if he'd even talked to her again.

He appreciated that no one brought up his last day in Sugar Creek but couldn't help but wonder if they blamed him as much as he blamed himself.

After another person walked over to welcome him home, Aaron allowed himself to bask in the glow of their acceptance. It felt good to be home, he realized as he headed over to the refreshment table for a drink.

He'd seen Amanda a few times during the day, but every time their gazes met, she rushed in the opposite direction. It was evident she was avoiding him, and Aaron couldn't help but wish that she would stop. He didn't want to bother her; he simply wanted an opportunity to tell her why he had left her at the altar. Until he explained to her what had been on his mind back then and in the years that followed, he wouldn't be able to move on.

After helping himself to a glass of orange juice, Aaron decided to track her down. This time if she walked away, he would follow her. He saw her with her sisters beneath a large tree, basking in the shade as young children played around them. As he approached her eyes widened and she shook her head, but that didn't deter him.

"Hullo everyone. Amanda? I was hoping we could go for a walk, to talk?" Aaron asked holding her gaze.

"I don't feel like a walk, and I have nothing to say to you." Amanda said firmly before taking Rose by the elbow and walking away.

Left with her eldest sister, Rowena, still supervising the children, Aaron let out a heavy sigh. "Any advice?"

Rowena smirked. "Don't leave a girl at the altar?"

Aaron shook his head. "Why do you think I need to talk to her? I need to explain to her why I left. I need to explain to her why I didn't come back sooner, but she simply won't give me the time of day. I know I was wrong; it kills me to know that I hurt her, but it kills me even more that she won't let me explain."

Rowena sighed. "If it kills you now, how do you think she felt in the months, nee, years, after you left without saying goodbye?"

"I know. It's just... I still love her Rowena. I know you might find that hard to believe but I do." Aaron admitted.

Rowena's eyes narrowed with curiosity. "You still love her? I'd have thought you ran away because you didn't love her."

"That wasn't why I ran. I ran *because* I loved her. I'd like to explain, but Amanda should be the first person I explain it to." Aaron kicked at the dirt. "She tells me she's engaged to the mann from the pet supply store at the flea market."

Rowena nodded. "Jah. They've been courting for the last year."

"Do you like him?" Aaron queried before he shook his head. "Sorry it was wrong of me to ask that."

"I do." Rowena shrugged. "He's nice enough. We're all just happy that Amanda has finally moved on. We were very concerned there for a while."

Aaron nodded. "I want to leave her in peace, but I need to tell her the truth. If she's happy, truly happy, then I won't bother her again. Is she? Truly happy?"

Rowena let out an impatient sigh and took a few steps towards Aaron. "You say you still love her?"

"Jah," Aaron answered without hesitation.

"And you won't hurt her again?" Rowena asked with a narrowed look.

"If it's within my power, I will never intentionally or unintention-ally hurt her ever again. I had my own reasons for leaving and it had nothing to do with her. Those reasons are something of the past now. Is she happy, Rowena."

Rowena paused for a moment and glanced at the children. When she met Aaron's gaze again, it reminded him of a lioness protecting her cub. "I'll only say this, Aaron. Do what you feel is right and follow your heart. But! And that's a big but, if you hurt my schweschder again, I will be the reason you leave Sugar Creek and never be welcome back here again." Rowena warned him with a narrowed look.

Aaron couldn't help the smile tugged at the corners of his mouth. Rowena didn't say her sister was happy, but she did encourage him to follow his heart.

She hadn't outright given him her blessing to pursue Amanda, but it was almost as good as a blessing, considering their past.

"Denke Rowena. Your kinner are cute."

Rowena laughed. "They're incorrigible, but denke."

Chapter 13
You Can't Run from Your Past

"Denke for coming," Amanda said handing the customer his change.

"My pleasure. I got all my doggy treats from Caleb. My pooches love it. Please tell Caleb I hope he feels better soon." The customer waved goodbye with a smile.

Amanda put the money in the small tin she kept separate for Caleb's sales. He had called her late yesterday afternoon to tell her that he was down with a terrible flu. Even through the phone, Amanda could hear his hoarse-sounding voice from all the coughing.

It was times like this when she wished he didn't live in the community on the other side of town. How she would've liked to be able to stop by and take him soup, or at least just check on him to show him that she cared. Except for not being close enough to stop by, Amanda didn't mind that Caleb lived in a different community at all.

In fact, she liked it.

Because, unlike everyone in her community, Caleb didn't know about her past. He didn't know how in love she had once been, and he hadn't been there for her being humiliated on what should've been the happiest day of her life.

And once they were married, she would leave her community and move to his. The idea of leaving her past behind gave Amanda some freedom to dream of her future. Although a lot of time had passed, Amanda still noticed the curiously sympathetic looks of the older ladies in their community. She could almost hear their thoughts as they watched.

Poor Amanda, first she was left at the altar and now she'll never find love again.

Luckily, she would prove them all wrong in a little more than two months. This time when she walked down the aisle her groom would wait for her. This time he would take her hand and he would be excited to commit to her.

Amanda pushed her thoughts aside and focused on the work at hand. Without Caleb there, she hoped it wasn't going to be too busy.

She didn't mind taking care of Caleb's stall as well, as the customers at the flea market were honest enough to bring their purchases over to her stall to pay. She had put up a sign that informed them that Caleb was absent for the day and that she was helping. That way, Caleb didn't lose any business and besides, he did the same when she was too ill to man her own stall.

Every now and then, between the lull in customers, Amanda's gaze would travel to Aaron's stall. For someone who was only in his third week as a vendor at the flea market, it seemed like his stall was a big hit amongst the customers. As if reading his market, he had begun making produce racks, unique coffee trays and other items that the Englischers simply doted on.

Rowena had talked to her at the community picnic and encouraged her to give Aaron an opportunity to explain why he had run from their wedding. Amanda had insisted his reasons didn't matter, but Rowena had said something that had stuck with her ever since.

Learning the truth would give her closure before she embraced her future with Caleb.

Now she couldn't help but wonder if her sister wasn't right. She had never gotten closure after being left at the altar and that day had never stopped haunting her. Perhaps hearing Aaron out will help her put that part of her life behind her so that she could move into her future with Caleb.

But deep down she feared listening to Aaron's reasons would excuse him rather than give her the closure that she needed.

"I'm sorry, could you maybe help me. I'm trying to find a leash, but I can't seem to find the right size." A woman asked nodding towards Caleb's stall.

"Of course." Amanda followed the woman back to Caleb's stall and after searching through the variety of leashes, found the right size.

She led the woman back to her stall to make payment, only to find Aaron assisting a customer with her products. He smiled at her over his shoulder before he focused on the customer again.

"This range is especially gut for sensitive skin. But if you want something that is more fragrant and moisturizing, then I'll try the geranium and cucumber range. It's refreshing, or at least, that's what my mamm says." Aaron laughed, saying almost exactly what Amanda would've said to the customer.

She assisted Caleb's customer with payment and then helped her own customer, who Aaron had encouraged to buy the entire geranium and cucumber range. Once her stall was clear of customers, she walked over to Aaron's stall. "That was nice of you, but they could've waited for me."

"I don't mind helping. I know you've got your hands full today." Aaron shrugged before he continued sanding a piece of wood that would become the handle of a coffee tray. "Is Caleb all right?"

"Jah, he's just recovering from the flu. I'm sure he'll be back by tomorrow." Amanda said reassuringly, but she stopped thinking of Caleb the moment she stopped talking about him.

Instead, she remembered the day of Abram's funeral. The urgency in Aaron's voice as he tried to talk to her. And every single time he had tried since. She couldn't imagine what he wanted to say to her that would change the way she felt about what had happened.

He had hurt and humiliated her. He had allowed her to dream just before crushing all her dreams in full view of the entire community.

Amanda stood there for a moment and heard her sister's voice of encouragement in her mind. "If you still want to talk to me, it would be best to do it here."

"Now?" Aaron asked, surprised, putting down the sanding paper and the piece of wood.

Amanda shook her head. "Not now. After closing. I have some time before the bus arrives, about ten to fifteen minutes."

"Or I could drive you home." Aaron offered eagerly.

Amanda immediately shook her head. The thought of riding in a buggy or a wagon, or any other form of transportation with Aaron wasn't a good idea. "Nee, after closing. I ride the bus home."

"Denke, I appreciate you finally giving me the time." Aaron said gratefully.

Amanda wanted to comment snidely about how he had wasted her time back then but decided against it. The purpose of their conversation was to get closure not to argue over something she couldn't change.

For the rest of the afternoon, she felt anxious about what he was going to say. She had no idea what excuse he had that would absolve him from what he did, she didn't think there was one that could.

She helped her customers, but her mind wasn't on her products or her sales at all. Instead, she kept her eye on the clock on the wall, waiting for the conversation Aaron should've had with her eight years ago.

When the bell rang, signaling that the flea market was closing for the day, her stomach was a ball of nerves. She slipped the piece of paper with a list of the items she had sold for Caleb into his tin, before summarizing her sales and income for the day in the book she brought with her every day.

Thanks to Aaron, her sales for the day were double what they usually were.

She had barely put her things in her basket that she would take home with her, when Aaron walked into her stall.

"Denke for giving me a chance to explain." He began with a nervous smile.

Amanda nodded, not wanting him to know how nervous she was. "You have fifteen minutes."

Aaron nodded. "Then I won't waste any of that time on pleasantries. There is a secret my family has kept for years, one that has never been shared. But you deserve to know the truth."

Amanda frowned. She had known Aaron since childhood, what could there be that she didn't know.

What was this family secret that had caused him to break her heart?

Chapter 14

Revealing Family Secrets

Aaron had practiced what he would say to Amanda for the last two hours and now that he stood in front of her, he was afraid to tell her the truth. He searched her gaze and knew that the Amanda he had known and loved wouldn't judge him for his decision, but she would understand.

He turned his back to her, knowing he wouldn't be able to admit the truth when she was searching for his gaze with pain in her eyes. "My daed was an abusive mann. And daed, ever since I can remember he physically abused my mamm. Luckily, her clothes always hid the bruises, or rather, he made sure not to hurt her where anyone could see. As the eldest, I took it upon myself to protect my schweschders from the wrath of his fists, but I couldn't always protect my mamm." The words were even more painful to admit than they had been to carry in his heart.

He heard Amanda gasp and felt her move closer to him. She rested a hand on his shoulder. "Aaron... I never knew."

"Because that's the way we wanted it to be. We knew if we told anyone, we would be punished for it. We kept it a secret, our family secret." He admitted bitterly.

"The week before our wedding... my mamm overcooked a beef roast. He went at her like never before. I intervened and managed to protect her, but not without landing a few blows myself. I beat him, Amanda... I made sure he was hurt for hurting my mamm or my schweschders again...." Aaron closed his eyes as he remembered that awful day. "It was wrong of me to submit to my anger, to raise my fists to my daed..."

"Aaron, you were protecting your mamm and your schweschders... Anyone would agree you did the right thing." Amanda said kindly as she moved in front of him and searched his gaze. "I would've agreed."

"That might be true, but you didn't know. I pinned him on the ground and vowed to kill him if he ever raised his hands to anyone in our familye again." Aaron said as a tear slipped down his cheek. "I went against everything I believed in Amanda; I threatened my own daed with murder..."

Amanda sighed and reached for his hand. "And you went through all this without telling me."

"How could I? I didn't want to tarnish you with the sins of my familye. With my sins..." Aaron admitted. "I loved you too much to drag you into that, Amanda."

Amanda was quiet, understanding and empathy evident in her gaze.

"That's why I had to leave. When I saw you on our wedding day, I was afraid that I would keep my word. I was afraid that I would marry you and then one day he would hurt my mamm or schweschders again and I would kill him. I was afraid that I would become the man that he was... I didn't want to hurt you that way. I couldn't stand it if I raised my hands to you, Amanda. I ran because it was the only way I knew I could protect you from the truth. It was the only way I could protect you from being married to me..."

"But you're not your daed, Aaron..." Amanda said quietly as a tear slipped over her cheek. "You're kind and thoughtful. You're loving and caring. You would never hurt me."

"But if I killed my daed, I would've been incarcerated and left you to live with the scandal," Aaron admitted. "I left because I couldn't do that to you. I spent the last eight years waiting for each letter, anxiously reading every word, waiting for the day he hurt them again. I don't know if it was because I was gone, or because he feared I would come back, but he never hurt them again. It took me standing over his grave to realize that I wasn't him. That I would never become him. There was something dark inside him, something that made him yield to anger instead of fighting against it. I don't have that darkness in me, Amanda." Aaron said holding her gaze.

"You've never been like that." Amanda agreed, squeezing his hand.

"And coming back here... I thought you'd be married, that you'd have moved on with your life. But when I saw you at the funeral... Amanda, I realized nothing has changed for me. I still love you like I did on our wedding day. I still dream of that future. I've never stopped loving you."

"Aaron." Amanda shook her head and took a step back. "I wish you told me all of this all those years ago. Things could've been different. I would've gone with you to Lancaster County. You didn't give me a choice back then and now... my choice has already been made. I'm getting married to Caleb."

Aaron nodded, having feared that would be her response. "I know. And if you truly love him like you once loved me and if you know he's going to make you happy, then I'll step aside Amanda. I love you enough to step back so that you can be happy. But Amanda... if you still feel anything for me... if learning the truth now, although I know it's too late, changes anything... I hope you'll give us another chance."

Amanda's eyes widened as she took another step back. "Aaron..."

"Don't say anything now, Amanda. I want you to search your heart before you answer me." Aaron said, taking a step towards her. "All I ask of you now is that you'll promise me you won't tell anyone what I've just told you. My daed is gone now, revealing the type of mann he used to be won't change anything, it will just humiliate my mamm."

Amanda nodded without hesitation. "Of course, Aaron. I won't tell anyone what you just told me. Just promise me one thing, regardless of what happens between us, you'll always remember that you're nothing like your daed. And what you did back then, you did out of love for your familye, not out of hate for your daed."

Aaron sighed. "I think I did hate him a little..."

"But you loved him as well, you loved him enough to leave." Amanda reminded him. "I have to go."

"I know." Aaron nodded holding her gaze. "Denke for listening Amanda. I should've trusted you enough to tell you the truth back then. I'm sorry that I didn't."

Amanda offered him a weak smile before she took her basket and headed for the exit.

Aaron watched her go and let out a heavy sigh. He had finally told Amanda the truth, now there was nothing left for him but to hope and pray that she still felt something for him somewhere in her heart.

Chapter 15

The Truth can be Devastating

A manda climbed onto the bus, struggling to hold back the tears.
For years she had simply accepted that Aaron hadn't loved
her enough to say, "I do." To now learn after all these years that he had
loved her too much, made her confused and angry.

If only he had told her what was going on in his life, with his family,
all those years ago. They could've been married and built a life together
in Lancaster County.

Instead, she had wasted years of her life on anger and self-doubt.
Wondering if she hadn't been good enough. Why he hadn't loved her
as much as she had loved him.

Her heart clenched at the family secret he had told her. Amanda
couldn't imagine being raised in a home where physical abuse was
doled out instead of love. She couldn't even begin to imagine how
difficult it must have been for Aaron, never mind his mother and
sisters. She wouldn't break her promise to him, their secret was safe
with her, but now that she had learned the painful truth, she wished
she could've been there for him.

It must have been hard for Aaron to walk away from her on their
wedding day. He thought this decision was the right way to protect
her. How lonely he must have been to move to Lancaster County,

leaving his family behind and the promising future they had dreamed of.

When the bus stopped at the start of the Amish community, Amanda climbed off.

"This isn't your stop?" A woman from the community asked Amanda curiously.

Amanda shook her head. "Nee, it isn't. But it's such a lovely day, I want to walk the rest of the way."

The woman looked at Amanda as if she had just grown two heads. She shook her head and walked in the opposite direction.

Away from the prying eyes of the people on the bus, Amanda allowed the tears to come. She was afraid if she held them back any longer, she would crumble as soon as she walked into the house. The last thing she needed was for her parents to ask why she was weeping. They would immediately think it was because of Aaron, but they wouldn't understand that she wasn't crying because of him, but for him.

She couldn't help but empathize with Aaron. She didn't blame him for raising his fists to his father, or threatening to kill him if he touched Aaron's mother or sisters again. In fact, she was proud of him for it. A mann who took joy in physically hurting others deserved anger and threats from his son, especially if it meant protecting others.

The truth about Aaron's decision to leave her at the altar struck deeper than she had thought it would. She had imagined his excuse would be something menial. Something along the lines of Aaron not being ready for commitment, or that he was too young, or that he first wanted to make something of himself.

But instead, the truth was much more disturbing than that.

Knowing that, and hearing that Aaron had never stopped loving her, confused Amanda completely. Learning that he hadn't walked away out of cowardice but rather out of respect, she couldn't help but find herself wondering what her life would've been like if she had known the truth. She and Aaron would've been married and probably have had a couple of children by now.

Her heart clenched at all that could have been.

But it completely stopped when she remembered Aaron's request.

Did she still love him?

Did she love Caleb the way she had loved Aaron?

Amanda stopped a short distance from her home and wiped her face clean of her tears. She took a few deep breaths, hoping the calm breathing would help rid her face of the red blotchiness.

As she glanced out over the horizon, Amanda feared she wasn't brave enough to search her heart for her true feelings. She feared that what she would discover would hurt Caleb, and although she now understood why Aaron broke her heart, she still didn't wish that on anyone.

Ever since she had been left standing alone on her wedding day, Amanda had feared falling in love again. She had kept herself guarded for years but she realized now that if she wanted the happiness the Lord promised in his word, she needed to be brave.

Brave and patient.

Patient for the Lord to show her the way and brave enough to follow it.

A bible verse came to mind, one that she had read numerous times before and it had never felt more applicable than in that moment.

Psalm 32:8 The Lord says, "I will guide you along the best pathway for your life. I will advise you and watch over you.

As Amanda walked into the yard of their homestead, she cast her eyes to the heavens and prayed for just that. Hopefully, with the Lord's guidance she would find her way to happiness after all.

Chapter 16

Patience is a Virtue

It felt as if a weight had been lifted from his shoulders. A weight he hadn't even realized he had been carrying for the last eight years.

Telling Amanda, the truth about what happened the week before their wedding had never been an option for Aaron. He hadn't only protected his family by keeping their secret, but he had protected his own pride.

Admitting that he had raised his fists against his father, that he had threatened his father with death and that he had left because he was afraid that he would be capable of it, were all things Aaron had believed would make Amanda hate him forever.

But evidently, he hadn't trusted Amanda like he should have.

There hadn't been disappointment in her eyes, or judgment in her voice. Instead, there had been nothing but understanding and support. How much easier that period of his life would've been if he had trusted Amanda enough to support him. He hadn't just let her down on the day he had walked out on their wedding, he had let himself down.

Amanda would've never blamed him, he realized now.

Eight years too late.

She would've supported him and stood by his side regardless of the troubles in his family.

A heavy sigh escaped him, realizing that he had done everything wrong.

Now, in retrospect, he feared that he had made the wrong choice all those years ago. He should've told Amanda the truth. He should've asked her to come with him.

Then they wouldn't have wasted the last eight years of their lives, and he wouldn't have to compete with Caleb Hauptfleisch for her heart.

He didn't want to be hopeful, because he feared if he had hope that Amanda still loved him, he would be crushed if she didn't. Now that he had revealed his feelings and the truth to her, Aaron couldn't imagine a future without her.

But that wasn't up to him.

She was engaged to another man and unless she came to him, Aaron had to do the right thing and step back.

The following morning when Aaron arrived at the flea market, Caleb was back in his stall. He watched as Caleb said something that made Amanda laugh, and his heart clenched with envy, making him catch his breath.

In that moment, Aaron knew that if Amanda went through with her wedding to Caleb, he wouldn't be able to stay in Sugar Creek. How could he stay and watch the woman he loved live a life with another man. How could he pretend to be happy when she had her first child, when he wanted nothing more than to be the father?

He walked into his stall and began sanding the coffee tray he had been working on the day before. His decision was made.

If Amanda didn't choose him, then he couldn't choose Sugar Creek.

He might have done everything wrong all those years ago, but this time he was going to do it right. The first step had been telling Amanda the truth. The second step was going to be a little harder. Now he needed to be patient.

He needed to give her time to process what he had told her, and he needed to give her time to search her heart. He could only pray that when she did, she would find him there.

Just perhaps, she would choose to dust off the feelings she had for him and embrace them once more, instead of choosing a man that had come after him.

Could Caleb even begin to comprehend the kind of love Aaron had for her?

Aaron didn't just love her, he admired her. He respected her and would give anything to see her happy.

A heavy sigh escaped him as he continued to sand the tray, even if it meant that happiness for Amanda meant choosing Caleb over him.

Her laughter carried into his stall once more, and Aaron gritted his teeth. He hadn't given her a timeframe, but how long would he have to be patient before he knew what she had decided.

A week, a month, or more?

The wedding was only two months away, Aaron reminded himself. He would wait until then.

Chapter 17

Nobody's Fool

Caleb didn't like staying home on flea market days. Except that it was his responsibility and provided his income, he didn't like putting the burden of his stall on Amanda.

But yesterday, he didn't really have a choice.

The flu had snuck up on him without warning and he had been in bed since Monday. Although he had felt much better the day before, he didn't want to come to the flea market and offend not only his customers, but other vendors with a hacking cough.

Instead, he'd stayed in bed and drank enough of his mother's snake juice that his cough had almost completely subsided.

Armed with a thermos of coffee and a few flowers he had picked in his mother's garden he headed straight to Amanda's stall when he arrived at the flea market.

He didn't know why but every time he saw the display rack that Aaron had made for her an uneasy feeling tickled his spine. He glanced towards Aaron's stall and assured himself he had nothing to be concerned about before walking into Amanda's stall. He found her on the ground, near the back of her stall, dusting the bottom shelves.

"Guten mayrie, mein liebe." Caleb greeted her with a bright smile.

She turned to him with a smile. "Caleb, guten mayrie. How are you feeling?" Amanda asked, coming to her feet.

"Much better, denke. My mamm's snake juice tastes terrible but it works like a charm." Caleb chuckled.

"That's gut to hear." Amanda smiled before her gaze was distracted by something behind him. Caleb turned and followed her gaze, only to see Aaron arriving at his stall. When he turned back towards Amanda he noticed that there was anger in her eyes like before but instead... almost melancholy?

It troubled Caleb more than he would admit.

"So how did yesterday go? I thought you could tell me over kaffe?" Caleb asked with a hopeful smile.

Amanda nodded with a smile, but it didn't reach her eyes like it did in the past. "Of course."

That was exactly what she did. She didn't talk to him about the wedding or anything for that matter, she only told him which purchases were made the day before and handed him the tin with his money.

Now and then she would glance towards Aaron's stall with almost curiosity before she turned her attention back to him. Caleb didn't want to be jealous, but it was hard not to be slightly envious of the way Amanda sought out Aaron whilst having coffee with him.

He tried to convince himself that Amanda and Aaron's past didn't matter, but suddenly he couldn't help but wonder if it did. Amanda had been very brief in her explanation about her past with Aaron, but now Caleb wondered if there was more to the story than Amanda had told him.

Ever since Aaron had taken a stall at the flea market things between him and Amanda had been a little different. He couldn't exactly put his finger on it, but Caleb knew it had to had something to do with the man from Amanda's past.

"I better finish dusting, if you'll excuse me. The last thing my customers want is products covered with dust." Amanda tried to make a joke, but Caleb caught on to the fact that she wasn't in the mood for his company.

He tried not to be offended by it, but as he walked back to his stall, he realized he hadn't even given her the flowers. He might be pretending that everything was fine between him and Amanda, but he wasn't anyone's fool.

Things weren't the same and they hadn't been since Aaron arrived. He couldn't be sure if it was because Amanda was disturbed by Aaron's presence, or if it was because she perhaps still had feelings for him.

Either way, Caleb promised himself that he would get to the bottom of it, sooner rather than later.

Chapter 18

The Truth comes in Different Flavors

With Caleb back in his stall today, Aaron made sure to steer clear of Amanda. After telling her the truth yesterday, he reasoned she needed the space, and to be honest, so did he.

He didn't want Amanda's sympathy and feared that if he saw her today, that was what he would get.

He only wanted her love; he thought as he made his way to the food court. His mind simply wasn't on his craft today and with it being a quiet day at the market, Aaron had occupied his hands by eating everything he had packed for lunch. He knew eating wasn't going to solve any of his problems, but for one day he would spoil himself by treating himself to a freshly baked soft pretzel.

"One cinnamon sugar pretzel, please." Aaron said to the lady behind the counter after perusing the variety of pretzels on display.

"Of course. Denke for your support." She handed him the pretzel in a serviette before accepting his money.

While Aaron tucked his wallet back into his pocket, Caleb arrived.

"A mustard pretzel and a poppy seed pretzel please." Caleb asked the lady.

A smile tugged at the corners of Aaron's mouth. "Poppy seed for Amanda? She's always loved poppy seed, although I don't even think it has a flavor."

Caleb nodded. "Me either."

Aaron started to walk away but Caleb quickly caught up with him. "Do you mind if we talked for a minute?"

Aaron could see in Caleb's eyes this wasn't going to be an assessment of the weather. "Sure, you want to head outside?"

"Jah, that would be best." Caleb nodded before they both headed towards one of the exits.

As soon as they were outside, Caleb turned to Aaron with a questioning look. "Amanda told me you and her have history?"

Aaron nodded. "Jah, we do."

"She told me that you were engaged to be married but you left?" Caleb asked to confirm Amanda's story.

Aaron nodded. "Leaving Amanda on our wedding day without an explanation was a terrible thing to do. I've regretted that day ever since."

Caleb's eyes widened with surprise. Amanda had left out the part about being left standing on her wedding day. "On your wedding day?"

"Jah, I'm not proud of it." Aaron sighed.

"Why did you come back?" Caleb asked the question that had been on his mind since first meeting Aaron. He didn't want to sound jealous, but he needed to know the truth.

"My daed passed away. I came back for the funeral... then I decided to stay." Aaron admitted holding Caleb's gaze.

Caleb let out a sigh of frustration. "I don't even know why I'm asking you this. I'm sorry if I'm being too forward. It's just... Amanda's been a little out of sorts since you've come back. I'm sure we're both just nervous about the wedding. It's nothing to do with you."

Caleb felt horrible for questioning Aaron and was about to head back inside when Aaron cleared his throat, making it clear he had something to add.

"Amanda is the reason that I stayed." Aaron admitted meeting his gaze head on.

Caleb's heart skipped a beat with fear. "Excuse me?"

Aaron took a step towards him with an apology and determination in his eyes. "When I saw Amanda at my daed's funeral... it was like no time had passed for me at all. I realized I still loved her, even after all this time. I don't want to deceive you as you look like a gut mann, so I'll be honest. If I had my way, Amanda would choose me. She'd forgive me for what I did all those years ago and we'd have the future we always dreamed of."

Caleb wanted to be furious, but how could it be when he was faced with such vulnerable honesty? "I...I love Amanda. Our wedding is in two months." Caleb said the words, knowing they sounded hollow at that moment.

Aaron shook his head. "And that's the problem, isn't it. Amanda loves you. I ruined my chance with her. Just promise me you'll take good care of her?"

Caleb nodded without hesitation. "I will. I promise."

"Then I guess there is nothing else for us to talk about." Aaron shrugged.

Caleb nodded before he followed Aaron back into the flea market. He hadn't expected such honesty from Aaron, or that he would feel sorry for the man that had broken Amanda's heart so many years before, but he did.

In his mind he had painted Aaron as the villain of Amanda's life, but now after talking to him, Caleb couldn't help but feel differently.

He could only hope that Aaron's return didn't change Amanda's feelings for him, but deep down he feared that it had.

Chapter 19

A Bogus Buggy Ride

Amanda had never been more grateful to leave the flea market than she was on Saturday afternoon. After being overwhelmed with the truth of what had happened eight years ago on Thursday, seeing Aaron every day hadn't been easy.

Add to that Caleb's constant kindness, confusing her even more about her feelings, she looked forward to a little distance from both men. Between working during the day and catching up with chores in the evenings she wasn't only physically, but mentally and emotionally exhausted as well.

She was even grateful that it was an off Sunday, which meant she didn't have to see Aaron at Sunday service either.

Eager to get home, she had begun to pack her basket and close her stall a few minutes before closing. This meant by the time the bell rang to announce the market was closed, she was ready to leave.

Amanda took her basket and walked out of her stall, only to be waited on by Caleb.

"Will five o'clock work for you?" Caleb asked with a hopeful smile.

Amanda frowned trying to remember if there was somewhere she needed to be. "Five o'clock?"

"I thought we could go on a buggy ride." Caleb shrugged with a hopeful smile. "Spend some time together away from the flea market.

The stretch from Saturday to Thursday is becoming way too long for me. But one of these days I'll see you every day." Caleb said, reaching for her hand. "Say jah?"

Amanda shook her head. "Nee, Caleb. Not today. I'm feeling a little under the weather." Amanda lied through her teeth. But what else could she say without offending Caleb.

Caleb let go of her hand, clearly her excuse had offended him anyway. "Are you sure you're feeling under weather or is it something else." Caleb glanced towards Aaron's stall. "Perhaps the blast from your past?"

Amanda's eyes widened. "Don't be ridiculous, Caleb."

"Am I though?" Caleb asked quietly. "Amanda, I can't help but feel that you've been distant these last few weeks. Even when we're together, it feels like your mind is somewhere else?"

Amanda closed her eyes, hating the guilt that made her cheeks flush red. She had thought that she had hidden her feelings and her confusion from Caleb, but clearly, she hadn't done a very good job of it. "Ach, it's just the wedding and the planning, and the stall... I'm just a little overwhelmed now."

"And your ex returning without warning, dredging up all those old feelings from when he left you at the altar?" Caleb asked with a cocked brow.

Amanda took a step back. "Actually, it was my parents' porch." She frowned; she hadn't told him that she had been left at the altar. "How did you find out about that?"

"It doesn't matter. What does matter is this growing distance between us. I'd like to think it has nothing to do with Aaron, but I can't help but feel that it does." Caleb asked, searching her gaze.

Amanda sighed. "Caleb, please. I don't want to argue. There is nothing between me and Aaron and there hasn't been since he walked away from our wedding. Just because I don't want to go on a buggy ride today, doesn't mean that I don't love you. I'm just feeling a little off and I'd like to go home and rest."

Caleb nodded. "So, you're sure this isn't about Aaron. Having him come back must've brought back some feelings?"

"Amanda, the bus is leaving!" a woman called out from the exit.

Amanda shook her head. "I must go. Have a gut weekend. I'll see you next Thursday."

Amanda escaped Caleb's questioning look before he could ask her anything else. She didn't want to lie to him, but she refused to admit that she had feelings for Aaron either.

Until she had time to search her own heart, she wasn't' ready to admit or deny anything. And until then, she wasn't ready to go on a buggy ride with Caleb and dream about their mutual future.

Because right now, Amanda realized as she took her seat on the bus, she wasn't even sure what her future looked like.

Chapter 20

A Mother and Son Moment

Saturday evening, it was just Aaron and his mother for dinner. They made dinner together and ate in silence before they washed the dishes side by side.

It still felt strange to be home without the constant tension and fear in the air. The fear that at any moment his father would lose his temper and Aaron and his mother would suffer from it.

"This is nice." Aaron said when they had done cleaning the kitchen.

His mother turned to him with a smile. "It is nice to have you home."

Since his father passed, neither Aaron nor his mother had spoken about what happened before he left. He didn't want to bring up the painful past, but he needed to state the obvious. "I meant it's nice not having daed around," Aaron admitted quietly.

His mother let out a quiet sigh. "Ach Aaron, I'm so sorry that you weren't here to see him after that night. Although his temper was still there, he never took it out on us again. He would rather spend hours walking in the fields than unleash his fists on me."

"I'm not sorry I left." Aaron pointed out.

"I am sorry that you felt that you had to. I know why you left, Aaron. I know your heart better than anyone else. And it wasn't to escape the situation or to protect Amanda from it, it was because you feared you would make gut on your promise." His mother searched his gaze and Aaron frowned.

"You knew?" Aaron asked with a frown.

His mother nodded. "Of course, I knew. That evening... it changed you. I've never said thank you, but I want you to know how grateful I am for what you did. That night, you gave up on the person who you had been until that point. I've never forgiven myself for that."

Aaron reached for his mother's hands and shook his head. "You have nothing to feel guilty for."

"But I do. If I had done something, spoken up, stood up against him, anything... I wouldn't have lost my son that night." Louisa said, biting back the tears.

Aaron hated that his father had resulted in his mother carrying the guilt for his actions. "Mamm, what could you have done. Divorce isn't permitted, you know that. And if you stood up against him, he would've struck you down even harder. He was responsible for his actions and for the events that followed. Not you. You never did anything to deserve the way he treated you."

Louisa sniffed and shook her head. "I've told myself that so many times and yet, I still struggle to believe it. The only option I had was to take you and your schweschders and leave the community. But how could I raise you in an Englisch world I knew nothing of, rob you of the heritage of being raised Amish."

"It's in the past now mamm, it's time for us to look to the future," Aaron said, pulling her into his arms. "We can't keep dwelling on what we could've done differently. It happened, but it's over now. He can't hurt you anymore."

Louisa nodded with a smile. "Denke seeh. If you look to your future, do you see it in Sugar Creek?"

Aaron let out a heavy sigh. "I want to say jah mamm, but it's not as simple as that."

"It's Amanda, isn't it?"

Aaron nodded. "How did you know?"

"Because I know you loved her enough to leave." Louisa said with a shake of her head. "It's not too late you know; she isn't married yet."

Aaron cocked a brow. "But she's in love with someone else. I spoke to her mamm, I asked her for another chance... I told her the truth."

Aaron expected his mother to be angered knowing that someone outside their family knew the truth about her husband's abuse. Instead, she smiled at Aaron. "You should've told her the truth back then."

"I didn't want to humiliate you mamm, and thinking back now, I don't think I was ready to share that secret."

"But you did now. I'll pray that everything works out the way it should." Louisa promised.

Aaron smiled. "Denke mamm. So will I."

Later that evening when Aaron turned in, he realized tonight had been the first time he and his mother had spoken openly about the past. Just a weight had been lifted from his shoulders after talking to Amanda, another weight was lifted now.

He might not know what the future would hold, but at least he knew he wouldn't go into it, carrying the weight of burdens from his past.

Chapter 21

The Fitting of the Heart

"Ach Amanda, I wasn't sure about the white. I was afraid it would make you looked a little washed out, but it's perfect." Sarah said as she pinned Amanda's hem.

Amanda smiled down at her mother. "It is, isn't it."

"Then why don't you seem happy about it?" her mother asked with a cocked brow when she came to her feet. "I don't want to bring up the past, but the last time we fitted your wedding dress, you were ecstatic. This morning... you seem almost nonchalant about it?"

Amanda let out a heavy sigh. "So much for not bringing up the past, then?"

Sarah framed her daughter's face and searched her eyes. "It's not wrong for a mamm to express concern over her dochder. Especially, a dochder that has had her heart broken in the past... What's going on?"

It was Monday morning and outside the birds were chirping while Rose did the laundry. For a moment Amanda watched her youngest sister and wished she could be as carefree as Rose. She had blamed Aaron for so many years for the scars he had left on her heart but now that she understood why, she couldn't be angry at him anymore.

She might have carried scars of that time, but Aaron carried so much more.

"Aaron and I talked." Amanda admitted quietly.

"You did? And what exactly does he have to say for himself?" Sarah asked with a hint of anger in her voice.

"He explained... his reasons mamm. And although I can't share them with you, I can't blame him for leaving. I can't be angry at him anymore. I wished he'd told me back then, but now that I know..." Amanda sighed. "I don't know."

"It sounds like you've forgiven him? It also sounds like you still have feelings for him, dochder?"

Amanda nodded. "I'm not sure I ever completely fell out of love with him. I tried to use my anger to hate him, but I realize now, it didn't work."

"And Caleb, what does he have to say about all of this? I couldn't help but notice you didn't go on a buggy ride on Saturday?"

Amanda shook her head. "Nee. We didn't. I think he's a little upset by that, but I needed some time to myself. I just feel so confused about everything mamm. About the past, about my future with Caleb, and about Aaron. I... I don't know what to do."

Sarah let out a heavy sigh as she took a seat at the table. Amanda joined her, not even considering the irony of having this conversation in her wedding dress.

"I don't want to see you get hurt again," Sarah admitted. "But I know when it comes to matters of the heart, we must be brave. We must embrace love as if it's a gift, one that can never tear us apart. I've never suffered the heartache you did, my dochder, and I hope I never will, but I just hope that you don't make any decisions based on fear. You must follow your heart."

Amanda let out a wry chuckle. "That's the problem isn't it, my heart says one thing and my head another. It's as if I'm being torn in two different directions."

"Does Aaron still have feelings for you then?"

"He asked me for another chance, mamm. He told me that if I really loved Caleb that he would leave and let me embrace my future with Caleb." Amanda admitted.

"That was... big of him." Sarah shrugged. "After making you question your feelings for Caleb..."

"What should I do mamm. You say I should follow my heart, but I fear I love Caleb and... I still love Aaron as well. I don't want to hurt either of them."

Sarah reached for her daughter's hand and offered support with a squeeze. "You should do what feels right in your heart. You should do what makes you happy. Forget about Aaron and Caleb and think of yourself. What will bring you joy, Amanda? If you close your eyes, with whom do you see a future?"

Amanda nodded. "Denke mamm. I have a lot to think about."

"Jah, you do. Just know, that I love you and whatever you decide, your daed and I will support you."

Amanda smiled gratefully. Her mother might support her and tell her to follow her heart, but that didn't mean Amanda was any closer to making a decision.

She glanced down at her wedding dress and wished that her feelings about her future fitted her as perfectly as her dress.

Chapter 22

A Torturous Tuesday

C aleb couldn't stand the uncertainty anymore.

Ever since Amanda had turned him down for a buggy ride on Saturday afternoon, he had doubts and fears circling in his mind. The more time he spent away from Amanda, the more he feared that the wedding they were preparing for wasn't going to take place.

Patience was what he needed, he realized as he priced new stock for the pet supply stall. But his patience was running thin. How much longer did he have to stand by and watch Amanda glance at Aaron with longing in her eyes?

How much longer did he have to wonder if she loved him the same way she did her first love?

By noon, Caleb decided it was time to talk to Amanda. He didn't know what he was going to say or how he was going to entice her to confirm her feelings for him, but he knew he needed to see her. The decision had been made, he realized, it was time to go and see his fiancée.

He arrived at the Flaud homestead an hour later. Amanda was helping her brother in the chicken coop and the surprised expression on her face when he approached them was exactly what he had hoped for.

He didn't want her to be prepared for the questions he had to ask, and he didn't want the answers she had thoughtfully constructed to spare his feelings.

He was after one thing, and that was the truth.

"Caleb? Did we arrange to meet today?" Amanda asked with a curious smile as she stepped out of the chicken coop. "I can't remember that we're going on a buggy ride. I'm not prepared at all."

"Nee." Caleb shook his head. "I thought I'd surprise you. I was hoping we could talk."

Her brother glanced at them, and Caleb held Amanda's gaze. "Alone."

Amanda nodded and headed to the water pump to wash her hands. He followed her around the barn to the willow where they had talked about their future in the past. Caleb sat on the fallen tree stump, wondering if it had always been there, and was dragged there for seating.

"What's on your mind?" Amanda asked with a smile. Although she acted like everything was fine, Caleb could see the anxiousness in her gaze. Her smile didn't reach her gaze.

"You." Caleb admitted. "You've been on my mind since Saturday. The more I think about you the more I realize that you haven't been the same since Aaron came back."

Amanda began to shake her head. "Caleb. Please, I don't want to argue."

Caleb nodded. "Neither do I. But I do need to know the truth. Do you still have feelings for him Amanda?"

Amanda let out a heavy sigh. "I didn't expect him to come back. I didn't expect him to explain why he left and the last thing I expected was to understand his reasons for leaving me at the altar." She didn't meet his gaze, but instead focused on the dirt beneath her feet.

Caleb refused to let fear override common sense. It didn't matter how hard this was, he had come for the truth, and it was the truth she had given him.

"When you look at him... I can't help but feel jealous. I don't think you've ever looked at me that way." Caleb admitted.

"Caleb, you know I love you." Amanda said quickly and reached for his hand.

Caleb smiled even as his heart was being torn into pieces. "I've never doubted that. But I also know that you love him differently... more somehow." Caleb let out a heavy sigh. "Amanda, although this hurts more than I can say, I need you to follow your heart. I love you too much to steal your future happiness from you. I need you to follow your heart and do what you know is right." Caleb reached for her hands and searched her gaze. "I know that if you do, your heart won't lead you to me. It might be your fear of getting hurt or even fear of being left at the altar again, but it won't be love. It's clear Aaron still loves you, and he seems like a gut man. If a man can leave you at the altar and give you a valid enough reason to still love him afterward, then you must love him. That isn't something any woman would just forgive... unless she loves a man."

Amanda's eyes widened before they glistened with tears. "I don't want to hurt you, Caleb."

"You'll hurt me more by marrying me out of fear. I don't regret our time together Amanda, you've taught me what it feels like to dream of the future, to love, and to embrace the moment. But I realize now that your future isn't with me. I should be angry, but I'm grateful I learn that now instead of after our wedding." Caleb assured her.

A tear slipped down Amanda's cheek. "I do love you."

"And you still can, as a friend." Caleb kissed her cheek. "I wish you and Aaron all the best Amanda. I hope that this time everything works out the way it should."

Caleb stood up, feeling heartbroken but relieved that he had learned the truth. "Gut bye Amanda."

***

Amanda watched Caleb walk away and felt a strange relief settle over her. She had feared hurting him the way Aaron had hurt her all those years ago and only realized now that was why she hadn't had the courage to search her own heart.

But now that he had made the choice for her in a way, helping her to understand her own feelings with his observations, she realized Caleb was right.

She still loved Aaron. She did see her future with Aaron.

And although she loved Caleb as well, Caleb had been right. She didn't love him the same way she loved Aaron.

A heavy sigh escaped her as she realized that she might have tried to convince herself that Aaron was in her past, but her feelings for him had always been present. Loving Caleb had been a way to try and embrace the future, and now she couldn't imagine the pain and the regret they would've both suffered in the long run.

She had always known that Caleb was a good man, that was why she had come to love him in the first place, but she hadn't realized what a good man he was until this moment.

To step aside for her to seek out her happiness with another man, was something only someone humble and brave would do.

She stared up at the willow leaves dancing in the wind and finally dared to look into her own heart. She might have loved Caleb, but she had been in love with Aaron since she was a young girl.

Caleb might have made her feel safe and cherished, but Aaron was the one that made her heart flutter and her knees quiver with excitement of what their future might hold.

Amanda could be furious over the years they had lost because he hadn't wanted to tell her his family secret, but how could she be angry when he had told her now. Aaron had told her the truth, knowing that she was engaged to be married. He had admitted his biggest mistake and asked her for forgiveness, knowing that she might still choose Caleb.

She no longer felt conflicted over loving two men, but instead, she felt grateful to have been blessed by having two such wonderful men in her life.

There would be a period of awkwardness between her and Caleb, but Amanda knew that in time they would once more be the friends they had been before they had started their courtship. Having a friend like Caleb was something she looked forward to.

And as for a future with Aaron...

The excitement that had lacked when she had fitted her wedding dress, suddenly washed over her like soap washing away the past, the pain, and the fear. Renewed with hope for her future and excited about everything it would hold, she walked away from the willow, knowing there was someone she had to go and see.

But before she did, she needed to tell her mother about the choice she had made. About the truth in her heart that Caleb had helped her to see.

Chapter 23

Packing up the Past

A manda still hadn't spoken to him.

Every day that he didn't hear from Amanda, made Aaron realize that he needed to accept the fact that in less than two months she would be marrying another man.

How could he not regret his actions in the past, if it meant that it would affect his entire future.

Aaron promised himself to stay until the wedding before he returned to Lancaster County, but this morning he woke up realizing he couldn't wait anymore.

How could he stay knowing that Amanda hadn't chosen him?

He wouldn't be a burden to her anymore. He wouldn't bother her with his presence, knowing that it only reminded her of the past.

It was time for him to take a step back and allow Amanda the future she deserved. A future that didn't include him, Aaron thought with a sigh.

He hadn't yet told his mother of his decision, but he would tonight over dinner. For now, he began to arrange the crates that had brought his tools and his crafts from Lancaster County, ready to repack them and have them shipped back to his uncle's homestead.

As he worked, he began to think about his own future. He would stay with his uncle until he found a place of his own. He would set up a workshop and dedicate his time and his attention to his craft. There wouldn't be courtship or a family, but at least he would have his craft.

Perhaps, in time, he would finally be able to move on, knowing that Amanda had a new life that he wasn't part of. One day, he might even be brave enough to fall in love again...

He huffed and shook his head, knowing that he would never love anyone as he loved Amanda. It would be wrong to commit to a woman, knowing that he couldn't love her the way she deserved.

It was time for Aaron to accept that he would remain a bachelor with only the memories of his time with Amanda to keep the loneliness at bay.

"Aaron?" his mother asked, finding him in the barn. "Someone is here to see you."

Aaron frowned. "Now?"

"Jah." His mother nodded. "I'll tell them where to find you."

Aaron let out an impatient sigh. The last thing he was in the mood for now was talking to a customer wanting to commission a project. Surely, that was the only reason someone would come to see him. He remembered the bishop's request and realized he hadn't been by to see the bishop yet, perhaps it was the bishop that had come to see him.

He dusted his hands on his pants and looked towards the entrance of the barn when footsteps approached.

It wasn't the bishop. It was Amanda.

"Amanda?" Aaron asked with a confused expression. "What are you doing here?"

Amanda shrugged. "I have a problem I hope you can help me with?"

Aaron moved towards her. He didn't want to solve her problems, he wanted to be the man she dedicated her life to. "I can try. What's the problem?"

AMANDA'S AMISH WEDDING   105

Amanda let out a heavy sigh as she shook her head. "I have this beautiful wedding dress, it's white and it fits me perfectly. I also have a trousseau chest filled with everything for my future. Then there are the guests that have already been invited and the food that's already been planned. But the problem is, I don't have a groom."

Aaron's heart skipped a beat as he took a step towards Amanda. "Caleb?"

Amanda's mouth curved into a smile. "He made me realize that I was too afraid to admit the truth."

"What truth?" Aaron asked as hope began to make his heart swell with love.

"That he's not the man I should be marrying. You see, it just so happens that I don't look at him the way I look at another man. He's not angry, we parted on good terms. We'll still be friends, but we both realized that it wouldn't be right to get married if the bride is in love with someone else."

"The wedding has been called off?" Aaron asked with a tentative smile.

Amanda shook her head. "Nee, that's the problem. Why call off a perfectly gut wedding just because I don't have a groom. Unless of course, you think you could step in at the last minute?"

Aaron's face exploded with joy as he rushed towards Amanda taking both her hands in his. "Are you asking me to marry you?"

Amanda shrugged. "Jah, but there is one condition though?"

"Anything?" Aaron asked as every single piece of his future fell into place.

"I'd like you to stay for this one."

Aaron swept her off her feet and spun her in a full circle before setting her down. He framed her face with his hands and searched her gaze. "I'm not going anywhere ever again. I love you Amanda, always have and always will."

"Gut, because I hear going through with a wedding is even more fun that just planning it." Amanda's laughter drifted through the barn.

Suddenly the past didn't matter, the fear vanished, and all the regrets Aaron had clung to disappeared. There was only him and Amanda, the way it should've been eight years ago.

Epilogue

"Then I hand the customer the harness, for a large dog, like he asked, and he holds it up in the air inspecting it as if it's wrong." Caleb said shaking his head, a hint of a grin touching his mouth. "He asks me if he can fit it before paying for it. Of course, I'm confused. There aren't pets allowed at the flea market and I'm not letting him take a leash and a harness, hoping he'll be honest enough to return to pay for it."

Everyone at the table listened avidly, eager to hear how the story ended.

"This is the best part." Rose, Amanda's youngest sister insisted.

"Before I can answer him, he calls over to his wife, who is holding the hand of their two-year-old son. This Englischer swiftly slips the harness over the boy's head, adjusts the straps and attaches the leash. Of course, I'm baffled. Stunned into silence." Caleb laughed. "It must have been evident that I was speechless at the sight of them leashing their son because he then continues to explain that his son is too curious for his own gut and runs off whenever they take their eyes off him for a moment."

"They leashed their seeh?" Aaron asked just as baffled at the story as Amanda.

"Jah. He paid for the leash and the harness and led his son away from my stall as if he were a dog. Luckily, the boy didn't start walking on all fours."

Laughter rung in the air as everyone envisioned a two-year-old wearing a dog harness and leash.

"Kumm, let's go serve dessert." Amanda smiled at her sister before she headed to the kitchen.

Rose joined her and took out the dessert bowls while Amanda served the chocolate baked pudding with cream. "And extra cream for Caleb, jah?"

"Jah, denke. I can almost swear that he loves cream more than he loves me." Rose laughed as she carried in the men's dessert.

Amanda picked up the bowls for her and Aaron and couldn't help but feel grateful for everything that had transpired over the last two years. It was hard to even imagine now that she had once thought that she and Caleb had a future together. Seeing him with Rose, only assured Amanda that everything happened for a reason.

She was meant to fall in love with Aaron. She hadn't yet figured out the reason for the eight years they had lost, but she was more than grateful that they had found their way back to each other. And she would always be grateful to Caleb who had the courage to show her the way.

As for Caleb and Rose finding love, that was another thing written in the stars before any of them realized what Gott's plan was.

It had happened while Amanda stayed home with her newborn son for three months. Rose had kindly offered to man the stall at the flea market during that time and before anyone realized what was going on, Rose and Caleb were in love.

Just like Amanda had predicted, things were a little awkward between her and Caleb after they called off the engagement, but not for long. They soon fell back into the friendship they had shared before their courtship. No one had been more overjoyed by Caleb and Rose's courtship than Amanda.

And surprisingly, when Rose and Caleb joined them for dinner the first time, Aaron and Caleb had become fast friends.

Nothing had transpired like Amanda had expected it to when Aaron had returned to Sugar Creek. Not only had she married the man she had always loved, but her friendship with Caleb had led to her sister finding her true love.

Amanda joined them at the table and handed Aaron his dessert.

"If Caleb loves cream more than he loves Rose, then I think I love this dessert more than I love you. Then again, I don't think it's possible to love anything more than I love you." Aaron reached for her hand and pressed a kiss to her palm. "Ich liebe dich, mein liebe."

The conversation circled back to the impending wedding of Caleb and Rose and Amanda couldn't help but be just as excited as the engaged couple about the big day.

She might have suffered through a humiliating experience on her first wedding day, but after having the perfect wedding day eight years later, Amanda knew firsthand how wonderful it felt to have the man you love commit to you for a lifetime without a hint of hesitation in his eyes.

"If you stand me up on our wedding day, I won't be as gracious to take you back." Rose playfully warned Caleb. "I'll hunt you down and kidnap you if I have to, but marrying you I am."

Caleb chuckled. "I won't be standing up unless it is to declare my love for you."

Amanda and Aaron shared a loving look, understanding each other's thoughts without even saying them out loud.

Their story hadn't been a usual one, it had been devastating at times and heartbreaking, but in the end their story had played out just like Gott had planned.

And if eight years apart had taught them anything, it was to seize every minute they had together.

The End

Thank you

Thank you kindly for choosing to read my book. I sincerely hope you enjoyed it. All of my Amish Romances are wholesome stories suitable for all to enjoy.

If you could be so kind as to leave a review on Amazon, I would appreciate it

Visit my Amazon Author Page for the complete list of books. While you're there, be sure to click on the "+ Follow" button on the left-hand side to receive new release updates directly from Amazon.

Also

by:

Amelia Yoder